MARK HALEGUA'S
THE BLUE LIGHT

BY NANCY HANSEN & LEE HOUSTON JR.

Airship 27 Productions

™

Mark Halegua's THE BLUE LIGHT
© 2022 Nancy Hansen & Lee Houston

Published by Airship 27 Productions
www.airship27.com
www.airship27hangar.com

Interior illustrations © 2022 Sam A. Salas
Cover illustration © 2022 Rob Davis

Editor: Ron Fortier
Associate Editor: Jonathan Sweet
Marketing and Promotions Manager: Michael Vance
Production designer: Rob Davis

ISBN: 978-1-953589-24-8

Printed in the United States of America

10 9 8 7 6 5 4 3 2 1

MARK HALEGUA'S
THE BLUE LIGHT

This manuscript was begun by our friend Mark Halegua, who left us unexpectedly and far too soon. Finishing it was a labor of love for both of us; a task filled with joy, a few shed tears, numerous ongoing discussions, and much dark chocolate consumed. One thing we all hope for as writers is that something we created will outlive us and become our legacy. Here's yours Mark, and thank you for sharing it with us, as well as trusting us to help guide you along the way.

—Nancy Hansen & Lee Houston Jr.

CHAPTER 1

Robert Ackers was just an ordinary man in his mid twenties, with black hair and wire rim spectacles over brown eyes, of average height and weight. Just another face in the crowd, he wandered along a 1931 Manhattan street rather distractedly, enjoying the early spring day. The sun was shining brightly in a clear blue sky. With the temperature somewhere in the sixties, he only needed a light brown outer jacket. He was thinking about a story he'd been working on when, from the opening of a nearby alley, he thought he saw a faint blue glow.

Since it didn't appear to be anything special, Ackers walked on by.

A block later he saw another glint of blue light.

Curious about seeing the same out of place phenomenon twice, this time he entered that alley and spotted a metallic object glinting with a faint blue glow lying on the ground.

Wondering what it could be, he picked it up.

It looked like some kind of medallion. Circular in shape, it was only three inches across with a radiant orb etched on one side with unusual writing around the edges. The other side bore a triangular, conical shaped impression with more unreadable writing around it. He flipped it over and over a few times like a coin, examining it and feeling its weight, which seemed heavier than it ought to be for something so small. Probably a foreign coin or souvenir.

Curiosity satisfied for the moment, Ackers put it in his jacket pocket and quickly forgot all about it.

Nothing came of this mundane act for a few days as he went about the usual responsibilities and tasks of his life.

Then he started hearing things.

Garbled words, low sounding like they were barely whispered. At first Ackers ignored it as unwanted background noise from outside his residence, either from the street below or one of the other units in the apartment building coming through the walls.

Day after day the noise increased as the words slowly become clearer, more distinct. Initially they sounded like random phrases in English. Then Ackers noticed they were beginning to resemble full sentences.

Becoming increasingly agitated, he feared the possibility that he was gradually going crazy and started losing sleep over it.

One afternoon, while sitting before the battered typewriter on his desk and working on a story he hoped to sell, he heard the sentence that would change his life.

"Hello Robert Ackers. Hello Robert Ackers. Hello Robert Ackers—"

Convinced by now that he was either potentially insane or someone was playing tricks on him, Ackers looked around. Yet all was as it should be in his small apartment. There was no one else nearby and no one to judge him.

With nothing to lose, he decided to answer. "Hello?" he said out loud.

"Ah, a response. Hello Robert. May call you Robert? That is your primary designation, is it not?"

"Um, well— sure. Why not? That's my name. Who are you?"

Looking around again and still seeing nothing, he added, "Where are you?"

"I will answer the last question first. I am in your pocket. Remember the blue metallic object you picked up a few days ago?"

"Yeah," Ackers said, vaguely recalling what then appeared to be just a random object.

"That is I, or should that be me? It took some time to become acclimated to you and establish communications. You do not actually 'hear' me, nor do you need to speak aloud in the way you normally converse with others. We are communicating telepathically."

"You're— in my pocket? We speak— telepathically?"

Confused, Robert went to the jacket hanging on a nearby wall hook and pulled out the medallion. In the room poorly lit by a single bulb in a ceiling fixture, the medallion still glowed slightly.

Turning the object around to look at both sides, it started glowing brighter and brighter until he dropped it as if his bare flesh might burn.

Now laying on the wooden floor, the 'sound' of the voice was fainter.

"I am not dangerous. I have just been in your pocket for so long that being out in the open felt— pleasant. You can pick me up without being injured."

Bending down, Robert tentatively picked up the medallion.

"Oh boy, would you look at me. Talking to a coin! How are you speaking to me?"

Louder now, the voice replied, *"Actually, since you have yet to accept everything I said, I am creating vibrations in the air for you to 'hear' with your auditory sensors. I believe you call them ears. But I prefer to communicate with you telepathically. I believe that is the correct term in your language. Also, I will be better 'heard' if you maintain contact with me.*

At least for now. That will change in time."

"Again with the 'telepathically' thing. Am I going crazy? Hallucinating?" he asked as he sat down again.

Robert Ackers 'heard' an emphatic *"No, you are not! You are in fact mentally healthy and stable, although you have become more agitated of late. I believe that is my fault."*

"Okay then. So I'm talking to myself." Ackers feared he'd lost control of his mind.

"How can I prove this to you? Ah... Perhaps if I alter my shape."

Ackers was surprised to hear this as the medallion 'spoke' further. *"Yes. I can change how I look,"* and with that reformed itself into a ring wrapped around one finger. That completely panicked Robert.

"Ahhhhhh! Get off get off get off get off!" he shouted, jumping up from his chair to frantically try removing the blue ring from his finger, dancing around the room like a madman in the unsuccessful process.

The object complied and reverted back to being a medallion. *"Robert please stop. I do not mean to cause you discomfort and apologize if you misconstrued my actions."*

Robert stopped moving, but placed the medallion on the desk. He was too overwhelmed to do anything but stare at it for a while as it gradually began to dim.

+++

The medallion broke the silence. *"Now that you have regained control of yourself, please pick me up. I am losing power that I need to communicate with you."*

That brought Ackers out of his reverie. "Look, I don't know what to think about all this. I'm scared that I'm hearing and seeing things that aren't there," he admitted aloud.

"You are doing neither. I am not sure how I can fully prove that to your satisfaction if you continue to overreact. I must warn you that if you do not stop shouting and jumping around, you will draw negative attention from other beings in this building. It is far easier for us to communicate silently, through your thoughts. Are you willing to pick me up and just pay attention so I can try to explain what I am?"

Looking desperately around the room, Robert took some small comfort in seeing nothing amiss, except maybe his sanity. Slowly he calmed down and then looked at the strange blue object. *Well, okay, I guess,* he thought.

Lifting the medallion once more, its blue glow slowly increased. *Heck, maybe this crazy moment will give me an idea for a story to sell.*

"Actually, that is one of the things that drew me to you."

I'm sorry. I don't understand, Robert admitted. *My writing drew you to me?* Most of the time it turned people away. But then this was a thing, not a person.

"Yes. My instructions were to look for an individual of imagination, along with one possessing an honorable character, generally good health, and mental stability."

Your... instructions?

"That is as close a term as I can describe. Your language does not have the proper vocabulary. I will need further exposure here to increase my knowledge base in hopes of communicating better, among my other tasks. The closest description I can come to that says what I am is what some describe as a computing machine. But that is terribly inadequate as well."

"Oh, so now I'm conversing with a machine. Wonderful," Ackers added aloud in a sarcastic tone. Scratching his head, he silently asked, *Exactly what is a computing machine?*

"A computing machine is one which can perform a series of mathematical calculations and data processing. It, I–"

Then the medallion paused. Ackers noticed the light grew a bit dim, as if the object had lost power again or perhaps was simply lost in thought, before it 'spoke' to him once more.

"This conversation is not proceeding properly. True, I am a machine. One which can execute any series of instructions to perform a specific task. In order to accurately perform these instructions, my chosen host—in this case you, Robert Ackers—must communicate with me as well. You indicate the task you want me to perform and I will attempt to do so. Those tasks can be simple or complex, mental or physical. I do have some limitations as to what I can accomplish, but the tasks can be somewhat abstract. For example, performing a series of mathematical operations, like adding a long list of numbers and giving you the result, or physical, like changing my shape, as you saw before."

I see. We're conversing telepathically now, so that is one type of mental task.

"Correct," the medallion replied.

You can perform mathematical operations? Let's try a simple one. What is 1,019 plus 2,133?

"3,152." The answer was immediate, with no hesitation.

Robert found a pencil and a piece of paper, then wrote down the numbers and performed the addition himself.

"Um, yes, that's correct," he conceded aloud, putting the paper and pencil on the desk near the medallion. "Hmm…" *A physical task. Can you write those numbers and the calculation on a piece of paper?*

As he watched, the medallion changed its shape into a ball and rolled across the desk before exuding a wire like tentacle which grasped the pencil and wrote on the paper the numbers and the answer.

Placing the pencil back into the cup, the tentacle receded. The ball then moved back into Robert's hand before resuming its original shape.

Robert stared at the paper. "That's—pretty darn incredible," he admitted aloud, though he was the only human in his apartment.

"Do you believe in me now?"

Raking his fingers through his black hair, Robert stared at the paper. *I just don't know what to believe. You're an amazing device. I can see you with my eyes but my mind keeps saying you're not real.*

"*You can change your thoughts to acceptance if you just let go of previously learned behaviors,*" the medallion voice counseled.

Easier said than done! Maybe if you tell me more about yourself. Where are you from? Who made you? What are you? Who gave you your instructions?

The medallion was noticeably silent, its light almost completely extinguished for a moment before saying, "*I cannot share that information.*"

You can't? Why not? Robert's mental voice sounded suspicious.

"*I—I cannot answer that question either. There is something preventing me from accessing parts of my memory storage area. In this particular case, it is the sectors where the data pertaining to these questions would be kept. For whatever reason, that information is securely locked away. Even from me.*"

I see. Well, actually, I don't see, nor do I understand.

The medallion dimmed for a moment, thinking again, before responding. "*The series of instructions which dictate how I work are, for reasons I cannot or currently do not know, not allowing me to access that information. I cannot tell you any more on that subject.*"

Well, can you tell me why you are here and communicating with me specifically?

"*My purpose is to assist a chosen host. Again, in this case, you. I can tell you have the combination of qualities which fit the command structure within me I was instructed to search for. I scanned many people for a lengthy period before you came along. You are a unique individual among those I encountered.*"

I am? In what way? And how are you to assist me? Assist with what? Robert had lots of questions.

"*First, you have the quality of open-mindedness. You are not limited by certain ways of thinking. If you see a truth or a fact previously unknown to you, you can and do accept it and adjust your thinking and ideas to that new knowledge. You have few biases, with most being in regards to personal tastes. You have resourcefulness and ingenuity beyond most others of your world. All of these things together make you unique. These are important to my instructions and made you a compatible host for me.*"

Host had a nice sound until Robert realized he hadn't been given much choice. He was about to say so as the medallion's voice went on.

"*As to assisting you, I can do so in various ways both mental and physical. I can enhance your health, allowing you to resist or to inure you to sickness. I can increase your ability to recover from any illness you may still succumb to. I'll assist you in recovering from injuries you may incur, and boost your physical strength and skills. I can and have already enhanced your senses and mental faculties somewhat. There are other improvements I will introduce over time. Of course I can provide information, and perhaps give you advice on actions you may want to take.*"

Ackers had to stop and think about everything the medallion revealed to him. When he 'spoke', again, Robert asked, *You're saying I will be healthier, stronger, and faster? Will I be smarter too?*

"*Within certain limitations, yes.*"

How are you able to do this? It was exciting, but also a little frightening.

"*Through the creation of a symbiotic bond with you. We will both benefit from this connection. You can initiate a separation at any time with no harmful effects other than I will no longer be able to provide you with further enhancement, nor will I be able to protect you from illness, disease, accident, or dangerous action. You will retain your current increased physical and mental capabilities. However, the longer I am separated from you, I will weaken and eventually become mostly dormant again.*"

Ackers wondered, *When will this process of enhancement begin?*

"*Actually, it started the day you picked me up. You may not have noticed yet, but your weight has shifted somewhat. You have become more athletically toned and stronger than you were before. Your muscles have received some small stimulation, and the extra weight you had in fatty tissue has been reduced. Also, your sight and hearing are improved. It will soon no longer be necessary for you to wear your vision correcting devices.*"

Well, that may explain why wearing my glasses lately has been kind of ineffective, Robert realized. *I see better without them already. I was afraid the prescription had gone out of date and I was going to have to get new ones. They're expensive!*

"In a few days they will no longer be necessary. Your eyesight will improve immensely. As for me, I have become more active and have been absorbing energy, which I could not do without a host connection. You are my catalyst. The longer I am with you the stronger I get and the more I can enhance you."

Where do you get this energy from? Me?

"No, from the light rays of the yellow star you call the sun, and from ambient energy and radiation in the atmosphere around this planet, much of it coming from space. I can also absorb other types of energy like heat, visible and invisible light. You do not suffer in any way from this process."

Although still standing until now, Roger had to sit down at his desk. *All of this is coming at me like a searchlight just turning on in my mind. Very sudden and blinding.*

"For that, I apologize."

That's okay. If our positions were reversed, I'm sure you'd feel the same way too. But what are we supposed to do now?

"I do not understand the question."

What is your purpose in... bonding with me? Why would you do all this? Have you done it before? When?

"I do this because it is in my instructions to do so. My purpose is to find a human with specific attributes to attach to and interact with that person. You fit the requirements. As for the other questions, I cannot respond. That part of my memory core is also locked and unavailable at this time."

That's a convenient answer, thought Robert. *Anytime I ask an important question, you can't answer it. How am I to trust you when you won't answer those questions that make me uneasy?*

"I can see how that may disturb you. And, it is not a matter of will not. I cannot. But, I ask you this, how do you come to trust anyone?"

Hmm... Trust is usually built over time, between people.

"Yes, but only between people? Is not trust also built up between humans and other species? For example, between humans and animals? I can see images in your head of four footed animals. Canines, felines, equines. I would like you to give this relationship some time, so you may learn to trust me. For us to trust each other."

You want us to establish a relationship? Usually a relationship is built between two people. Yet, you aren't a person, Robert reminded the medallion. *You refer to yourself as I, which indicates some sort of self* awareness. You seem to have an intelligence, but you are clearly, from what I can see, manufactured. A device and not a being.

"Are you not also manufactured?"

Robert's eyes widened and his mouth opened in surprise. *WHAT? No! I'm a person, not built in some factory or laboratory!*

"True, but, you are a biological machine. You intake fuel to run your body and excrete waste. You respond to your surroundings with sensors of various types. How is that different than what I am doing?"

Well, because I am— biological, I'm not manufactured, I'm born. A male and female of my species breed and from the two of them a baby is created who, over time, grows and learns and matures.

"And you believe I have been 'born' in a different way?"

Well… began Robert, trying to figure out how exactly to respond. Even with some of his science fiction writing he had never considered creating a device that became sentient and had magical abilities. *I don't really know what to believe.*

CHAPTER 2

After a long debate on what did and did not constitute life and existence, which failed to reach a satisfactory conclusion, Robert Ackers and the medallion lived in relative peace for a while. He kept it with him and in turn, the blue object remained relatively quiet.

Then one day Ackers made a pivotal decision.

Okay, you're bound to have a lot of energy stored up by now, he said in a thought directed at the medallion as he lifted it up. *I'm curious about what we can do together. Let's try a few things.*

"What kind of things Robert?"

Things that might help others. If you can do everything you say you can for me, I want to put those abilities to good use. But when I do so, I don't want to be recognized.

"Why not?"

Because I'm not officially authorized to do certain things. I'm what's called a civilian, not a law enforcement officer or someone in the military, so technically I have limited rights to act on the public's behalf. I might get arrested for interfering, he explained. *Also, if I can be identified by certain people in the crime underworld, they could try to hurt or even kill me or* other people I know. So anonymity is the best thing for me and you.

"I understand. So you are more acceptable if you remain anonymous?"

No, but if I can't be recognized, it will be safer for us and the people around me.

"Is this sort of intervention illegal in your world?"

There's no direct regulation against it, but it is frowned upon, Ackers replied truthfully. We pay specially trained people to do these things, but they can't be everywhere. And some of them can be corrupted or threatened so that they don't do what they're supposed to. Everyone will be a lot safer if no one knows who I am.

"Well, I can project a field around you that will provide both that anonymity and partially shield you from harm."

All right, do it now! Ackers insisted. He was eager to find out what it would feel like to have such powers.

Before the last syllable was completed, Robert Ackers was surrounded by a blue glow that covered every inch of his body. He walked over to a full length mirror in the bedroom and looked at himself. In the reflective surface was a larger, almost seven foot tall, husky humanoid shape. There were no discernible features, just blank blue light, although he could just faintly make out a darker man's outline deep within.

That works nicely. I can see perfectly, and the surrounding aura hides my whole body except for the general shape of a person. You'd have to disguise my voice though, or someone might recognize that if I had to speak. But hey, why am I blue? he asked the medallion.

"That particular hue just comes naturally to me."

Okay. But you said you can only partially protect me? Why only partially?

"As previously stated, I cannot fully absorb kinetic energy, so physical objects can do some harm. I can absorb almost any form of energy to an extent, although I will at times need to relieve excess energy. I do have a maximum capacity in regards to any specific function."

You can't just take in more? Ackers wondered. Like, I usually stop eating when I'm full, but that doesn't mean I'm incapable of at least attempting to consume additional food.

"I am unable to exceed my maximum storage capacity."

But what happens if you become overfull? Or go beyond your maximum?

"If I ever find myself at risk of being overcharged, I excrete the excess as a burst of light. Beyond that, I do not know to what extent I can safely contain excess energy. I cannot recall ever being in that state."

Okay. We'll need to reexamine that at another time, Robert conceded.

What else can I do in this form?

"*You can have me change the shape of the field to various solid forms.*"

Does that include the shape of the arms, legs, and hands?

"*Yes. Almost anything you can think of, I can do. However, the more complex the shape, the more energy I use.*"

Okay. Change the shape of the right hand to a scoop, large, about two feet wide, two feet long, with a flat edge in front. Use both appendages.

The two arms extend and joined together, then curved to perfectly form the desired shape.

Nice. Now can you form a moving fan or propeller?

"*Yes. Just remember that forming any mobile item uses more energy than a static artifact.*"

The two arms separated and then transformed to the required forms.

Good. Now, in all probability we'll be involved in confrontations of various kinds. Criminals usually will have some sort of weapon, Ackers explained. *You have an issue absorbing kinetic energy, and most weapons they use employ some variety of brute force, which is a form of kinetic energy. So things like pipes, crowbars, bats, saps, firearms.* He pictured each one in turn. *Other items would be sharp edged and pointed, like knives.*

"*These knives. They are powered by the person and not projected by an explosive weapon, like a firearm?*"

Robert confirmed that.

"*Then I can protect you from those without much of a problem. The field can either entrap and hold such things or deflect them. However, if they are pushed by an extreme amount of kinetic energy, they could penetrate to a depth within the field which might injure you.*"

You've been gathering energy for about four weeks now. Are you fully charged?

"*No. I am far more than I was though. Why do you ask?*"

I just think it would be a good idea if I were able to check on your power levels when needed. It might come in handy. After all, when we do something, doesn't it use up energy? Won't there be a situation where you might be almost empty? That could endanger both of us, Ackers realized.

"*When I use a lot of energy, it does lower my available energy for other tasks. I can give you a mental image of a capacity gauge, which would show my power levels. Would that suit you?*"

Yes, I think so. Studying it over time would also give me an idea of what specific functions drain you faster or slower. I'm sure there are things you do which don't use a lot of energy, like performing mathematical calculations and others which use a lot, like projecting the blue light body and other more physical tasks.

"That is a reasonable assumption," the medallion agreed.

Ackers was becoming enthused. He'd always wanted to know what it would be like to fight crime like the heroes he wrote about. *When can we try this out?* He asked eagerly.

"*Take me with you whenever you go out, and perhaps you will find a situation we can use as a trial run,*" the medallion suggested. "*I will charge far faster if we remain together,*" it reminded him.

From that day forward, when Robert Ackers went out, the medallion was always in a pocket.

+++

The opportunity came a month later. Robert was on his way home when he heard distressed screams and ran to where he saw two armed men chase someone into what he knew was a blind alley. "Something no good is going on back there," he muttered as he hesitated, not sure what to do. He checked his wristwatch and saw it was late. The primary thing on his mind had been going home to get a good night's sleep. It was getting chilly out too. Dressed in a light overcoat, he looked in both directions of the well illuminated avenue and then turned right towards his apartment.

The medallion was quick to respond. "*Robert, I can tell by the rise in your respiration and other chemical levels that you are agitated by the thought of danger to others. Perhaps this is a situation that we could investigate and finally test our bond.*"

Ackers realized the medallion was right. *Good idea,* he said silently. *But let me get in there first before we get too involved.*

"I will await your decision," the medallion promised as Ackers stepped into the darkened alley. Cautiously he stalked along until he heard up ahead a low voiced exchange and the clicking of a hammer pulled back that told him there were innocent people in imminent danger.

Okay, light me up. And don't forget to disguise my voice!

The dark alley suddenly became very bright, revealing it was littered with empty crates, overflowing trash cans, papers and other refuse. Everything was illuminated with a bright blue glow, including a young couple who had been backed into a wall, clutching each other fearfully.

Threatening them were two thugs wearing grubby flat caps and black leather, their jackets open to reveal stained turtleneck sweaters. Both men had loaded revolvers aimed at the couple, their free hands now shading their eyes from the strong light.

From the center of the blue glow a flat, mechanical sounding voice said, "I'd put down your guns and get out of here. You don't want any part of me."

One crook yelled back, "Yeah, well you ain't us. Shoot 'im Eddie!"

Gunfire echoed in the alley as the thugs tried to extinguish the light.

The bullets struck the blue light, seemingly forcing it back, though only a little.

While accurately fired, the projectiles never completely penetrated beyond the surface, stopping as if stuck in the glow like fruit suspended in gelatin. Then they were simply squeezed out and fell to the ground. The guns made clicking sounds as the firing pins hit empty cartridges in the revolvers' ammunition chambers.

The rattled gunmen, still pulling the triggers on their now useless weapons, stared at the sight before them, their eyes wide in shocked surprise.

The blue glow gradually moved toward them. The incandescence was shaped like a very tall, large human with a darker form inside, all features hidden by the too bright light.

The arms moved outward rather woodenly but still managed to slap the guns from the stunned thugs' hands. Then one hand split into two fists and struck each man in the jaw. They both fell to the ground, out cold.

The light turned toward the young couple, still clutching each other as they witnessed wide eyed and unbelieving this startling turn of events. They tried to retreat from the light as it moved closer, but were stopped by the wall behind them.

The voice emanating from the light said, "Don't be afraid. I won't hurt you. The police will be here soon. Just tell them what you saw."

The man stared and said, "W-what we saw? I'm not fully sure what we saw as it is! You want me to tell them some blue light man came out of nowhere and knocked those thugs who wanted to rob us out cold after they shot at it multiple times?"

"I like that," said the mechanical voice as sirens sounded in the distance. Someone had heard those gunshots and called the cops. "Yes. Tell them that. Tell them it was the Blue Light. Tell them that he— that I'll be around."

+++

The man with the blue glow surrounding him turned and walked more rapidly back to the end of the alley until he was out of the couple's sight.

After taking a quick look around to make sure no one was present, he thought rather than said, *Okay, turn off the light.*

With that mental command the blue aura around Robert Ackers winked out and he walked rapidly away down the street. After the alley adventure, he was feeling rather cocky and very elated.

Wow! What a rush! thought Ackers. *Hey, what gives with the bullets? They stung.*

"I have stated this before Robert," he heard the reply in his mind. "*I can generate a field around you that will inhibit the force of the projectiles, however I cannot completely stop them. They did not penetrate fully but I could not totally absorb the kinetic energy of their movement. I will become stronger than I am now, but you may want to avoid heavier projectiles with more force behind them in the future.*"

I'll keep that in mind whenever I walk into a situation where I have no idea what I'll be facing, Ackers replied. *This other thing, where you can 'enhance' my senses somewhat, is great. I was able to hear that couple's screams a couple of blocks away and I ran there faster than I ever could before,* he boasted. *I could clearly see the entire situation in that faintly lit alleyway almost as well as if it was daylight. And those crooks—boy, were they ever surprised!*

"Your body is registering higher levels of some chemicals. You are more alert than normal, and your blood pressure is still somewhat elevated, although returning to base quickly. Is this normal after such encounters?" the voice in his head asked.

Yes. Human beings have what is called a 'fight or flight' reaction built into their brains, for situations which may cause us harm. We either run away or, if circumstances don't allow for flight or for other reasons we decide to stay, we stand and fight.

"In this case you ran TO the dangerous situation. Inserting yourself where you could be hurt or killed. Is this one of those other reasons?"

Yes. There are among the populace those who work in public service jobs, like policemen, firemen, soldiers, and the like. They are essentially protectors whose responsibility it is to rush into dangerous situations to protect the rest of us. Uh, hold on. Do you hear that?

"No, I only notice what you tell me. What did you hear?"

It sounded like a crash. A couple of blocks in that direction. Robert pointed down one avenue and started running rapidly toward it.

+++

He spotted a crowd up ahead and stopped. They were gathering around two vehicles piled against each other. One was a delivery truck. The driver stumbled out of it with only a few scrapes and blood coming from a head wound, but otherwise seemed okay.

The other vehicle was a passenger car with three occupants: a man, a woman, and a child. All were at least stunned, if not unconscious.

As he watched, a small flame flickered to life from the rear of the car and grew larger by the second.

A woman screamed, "It's going to explode!" as the crowd scattered away from the crash site. The truck driver looked over at it and then haltingly limped away to safety.

Ackers took a step back from the crowd and began silently 'talking' to the medallion.

There's no way emergency crews are going to get here before that car explodes. Can the field you put around me protect me from the heat of the fire? Can I grasp objects? Can it protect anyone I'm holding? Can-

"*Please, give me a moment to answer some of your inquiries before I respond to others,*" pleaded the medallion. "*The field can absorb some of the heat energy and once you touch someone or something, you can bring that object or person inside your field and they will have the same protection you do,*" his companion silently replied. "*However, if there is an explosion, I do not know how much protection the field will offer from the concussive force. As I have explained, kinetic energy is much more difficult to absorb. In part because of the varying speeds involved versus whatever the nature of that energy source is.*"

Nodding, Ackers thought, *Yeah, okay, I understand. Now light me up.*

The blue field surrounded him and enlarged to almost seven feet as it hid his features within the bright light. He rushed to the passenger side of the car, drawing the attention of every onlooker who wondered who this new arrival was and where he came from.

Blue Light tried to open the front door to get the woman, but—

"The door's jammed! I can't pull it open!" he said aloud in his public monotone voice, as much for the benefit of those around him as the medallion.

Ackers punched his hand through the window, cleared the glass and pulled the woman out the newly created opening. Doing the same thing with the rear door window, he pulled the child through and carried both of them to safety.

As he returned to the car, the flames had grown larger and hotter.

Everyone feared an imminent gas tank explosion and stepped further back from the spectacle, except for a very anxious and shaky Robert Ackers, who as the Blue Light was completely unrecognizable.

With wonderment, Robert realized, *I don't feel the heat at all, but that poor guy must be frying alive in there!* That gave him the courage to continue.

Pulling at the driver's side door he saw it wouldn't budge either. Looking through the already broken window, Robert realized the man was too big and brawny to rescue that way.

Change my right arm to a large screwdriver, flat head shape, like the image in my mind, he instructed the medallion, which instantly complied with Ackers' request.

The field around his right hand formed a blue lighted extension with a sharp edge.

He punched his hand forward and wedged it inside the door jam, leveraging hard against the extension. With a screech of tortured metal, he forced the car door open on its hinges.

That should give me the leverage to open it the rest of the way. Change the field back to normal hand shape. Every word was rapid bits of thought and he had to focus hard on the task at hand not to lose his nerve and run off, leaving the trapped and unconscious man to his fate.

With tremendous effort, he grabbed the door edge and yanked with all his might. With a groaning and screeching sound the door opening widened enough to drag the man out.

Robert turned from the car and staggered away with the limp form of the much heavier man when, with a flash and a roar, the car exploded!

The power of the blast threw both of them forward and they hit the street pavement.

For a few seconds they didn't move and the blue light surrounding them dimmed.

Then the light gradually glowed brighter.

The blue lit figure rose unsteadily, then scooped up the still unconscious driver and stumbled over to set him down next to the woman and the child on the sidewalk around the corner from the burning vehicle.

"Will they be alright?" Robert asked aloud in a shaking tone, not caring if anyone else heard that specific question.

"I sense no serious injuries," was the silent reply. *"The man has some burns, but, yes he should survive. After a small amount of time they will all recuperate completely."*

A fire engine, its sirens screaming, rounded a corner and stopped. Men dressed in fire helmets and other protective gear leapt from the truck, efficiently unrolling hoses to connect them to fire hydrants. One fireman walked over to the glowing blue light, staring at it in stunned silence, before seeing the man-like shape within.

An ambulance and a police car screamed to a stop. The ambulance driver and his assistant hesitantly moved around the large man shaped light to the three lying on the sidewalk and began examining them. People were already talking to the officers now on the scene, telling them about how the Blue Light man saved those in the car from certain death. The police waved the crowd back so the ambulance crew could do their work.

One of the officers walked over, stared at the lighted figure, and turned to a woman standing nearby. "Does anyone know what happened here?"

"Yes. There was an accident, a car and a truck. Those three were in the car," a flat mechanical voice coming from the light said.

The officer turned in surprise. "You can talk? Who are you? How did they get out of the car?"

From across the street, one of the men from the crowd yelled, "We just told yah, the Blue Light pulled them out. He, uh— it was caught in the explosion when he pulled the man out. He protected the guy. He's a regular superhero, just like in them dime magazines!"

The officer turned back to the large glowing man thing. "This blue light did all that? Well I guess they owe you some thanks. Are you all right? You didn't get hurt from the explosion?"

"I'll be fine." Robert Ackers' mechanical voice sounded a little stuffy even to him, but then, they couldn't see that he had teared up.

Another police officer walked over to stare at the Blue Light. Then turned to the three lying on the sidewalk with the ambulance attendants looming over them, before facing the light again.

"I, hmm— Well I need to ask you some questions for my report. I, that is, um, what's your name?"

"You can call me Blue Light."

"Blue Light. Riiight. What's your real name pal? Where do you live? That is, in case we have any other questions we need to ask?"

"Just Blue Light. I need to go now."

With that, Blue Light turned and ran more rapidly than any human could run. He was down the street and had rounded the next corner before the officer could move to pursue him. Or it. Whatever it was!

+++

"Are you all right?"

"WOW! That was— just incredible!" Robert Ackers said aloud, enjoying both the moment and the feeling of accomplishment.

He looked around and saw no one in the immediate area, but feared the officers or someone else might come after him with more questions. *Okay, you better turn the light off. I don't want to attract any more attention,* he silently instructed his companion.

The medallion complied while saying, *"As before, some of your bodily functions have risen to higher levels which are now returning to normal. Your blood pressure, adrenal glands, and more. Probably from your actions moving those people out of a potential harmful circumstance. Is this one of those situations where you fight instead of flee?"*

Yes. I acted to protect those people.

"Your actions also put you into a potentially dangerous situation. However, my response to it is… I believe you acted appropriately. I… feel… a response I am not sure how to express."

Is this feeling a positive or a negative one?

"It is positive."

It was for me too. I got a little emotional there toward the end. So, you're going to help me to continue helping others, even if I wind up placing myself into dangerous circumstances in the process?

"It is your intention to continue on this path? If so, then… yes. As long as you do not personally benefit from these actions in any way."

Robert smiled. *That's what heroes do, and you have made it possible for me to be a hero twice today,* he was thinking as he wearily headed home. *I now have capabilities, with your aid, beyond what I ever had before. I can help people in ways I could only dream of and write about before. If I can continue to do that; if I can help people, save lives, make this little part of my world a better place— then yes. I want to continue as the Blue Light.*

CHAPTER 3

Clack, clack, clack.

The typewriter sound was a steady staccato beat as Robert pounded the keyboard the next day.

"You are writing something. A new story? Why?" his companion asked in their unique way that only Robert could hear.

It's how I make money, writing fiction for magazines. This story is for one of the scientific fiction mags, Ackers mentally answered, privately proud that he had mastered 'talking' with the medallion that was currently sitting next to his typewriter. *Please hold on while I finish this page,* he requested.

"*Hold on to what?*" the medallion asked in return.

Robert just frowned and resumed typing. When he finished the page, Ackers moved the paper out of the roller. Separating the copy below from the original above, he placed both face down onto their respective piles next to the machine. The carbon paper he set aside, hoping to be able to use it again.

Now then. You have questions for me?

"*Yes. Why do you need to make money? I do not understand the concept of money here.*"

I need money to pay the bills. Rent for the apartment, to buy food, to travel and socialize with others, that kind of thing.

"*Money is a method of exchange? You do not exchange services for other items? Is there not a method of barter?*"

Well, money is a way for people to exchange services in a sense, Ackers thought hard about how to explain it. *I sell my stories to a magazine publisher and he prints them so interested people will buy the magazine for entertainment or information. It's a way for me to make the story available to a large audience. This way I don't need to barter it with every individual who may be interested.*

"*But would not bartering be easier?*" the medallion asked.

No. For one thing, I don't know everyone who might be interested. Also, the people who might be interested in it may be widely separated geographically. Another reason is I may not need all the services the readers might be able to provide. Some of the readers may work on a farm, in a store, in a factory, or an office of some kind. They earn money in their way and pay some of that for the magazine. The publisher accumulates that money, then pays for the printing, editorial services, artists, and me for the story. Hopefully, he makes a profit which allows him to continue publishing, and there are many people who benefit from this success. You don't see that in my mind?

"*I have been trying not to intrude in your mind when either uninvited or unneeded. You need to think of something specific and direct that thought at me now for me to understand your ways. Even before I was only able to gather surface thoughts. Those were not always orderly. Sometimes your thoughts were so rapidly changing I could not understand them. Then there were other, more ethereal items I could not interpret.*"

But you had to intrude more deeply in my mind in order to begin communications, Ackers reminded his companion.

"Not really. I was able to learn by observing you communicate with others. I could do that without being intrusive. I observed you giving metallic and paper objects to others and getting something for those transactions, but did not completely understand the meaning of the action."

That was money. I was exchanging what I earned for the goods and services I needed.

"I understand the concept better now. Does everyone earn this money they acquire."

Most honest people do.

"Honest? Please explain the concept of honest."

That was going to be tough, because it was so subjective. Honesty had a lot of nuances.

I've briefly mentioned this before, back when we were talking about why I needed to disguise myself, recalled Robert. *Honesty is where a person performs a task and is paid for it. Some people try to take what they want from others instead of earning it. That's called stealing. It's dishonest. They didn't earn either the money or the item.*

"I understand. There are dishonest people. Does this happen often?"

More often than is good. There are many people who perform in a dishonest manner to acquire money or other items of value, some of which they convert to money or power, the ability to control the actions or circumstances of others. They're called criminals.

"Some of the people I scanned for a potential host had traits I did not like. Was that this dishonesty? How are they prevented from performing their dishonest acts?"

I can't answer whether they were dishonest or criminal in their thoughts because I wasn't with you then and can't read their minds. And various forms of police agencies enforce laws made to punish these acts.

"What are laws and how are they decided?"

Robert pondered this question and then replied, *I think we've discussed this enough for now. I can answer more questions later. Right now I'm hungry and want to go to the diner for a sandwich and a soda. But first, I have a question for you.*

"Ask and I shall respond if possible."

You've repeatedly used the noun 'I' when referring to yourself. It's natural for me to do so in my native tongue, English. It's a form of self-awareness. Are you self-aware?

"Self-aware? Yes, I suppose I am. I think, therefore I am."

Robert laughed silently. *There is a Latin phrase a smart person, a philosopher named René Descartes, used to describe the same thing. Cogito ergo sum.*

"I see. What is this Latin? And as for your hunger, you have felt this hunger before. It is your body's way of saying you need to intake energy to continue, correct?"

Yes. Changing the subject again, I see. Okay, we'll converse more about that later. I want to go out today instead of eating here like I usually do. I can stretch my legs, get some fresh air, and socialize a bit. The diner has people. You can watch them while I eat and maybe learn something. You're like a newborn who absorbs all it experiences. Didn't you learn a lot while waiting for the right person to pick you up?

"I was mostly dormant. I only had the basic energy to sense when the right person came along. Only after you claimed me was I able to absorb more energy and start communicating with you. Especially after our recent excursions, I am still not at full strength yet, but getting stronger. Therefore, I am now able to direct my attention to acquiring more information from my surroundings."

Then let's go feed both of us, so to speak, Robert thought smugly, before grabbing the medallion and putting it in his shirt pocket.

+++

After securing his apartment and heading down the tenement stairs, Robert heard a loud crash and incoherent shouting from a slightly open door on the first floor.

Running toward the door Robert 'said' to the medallion, *That's my landlady's apartment. Who's she yelling at?*

He rushed into the room and saw a large man raising a gun in one hand while using his other to protect his head from a thrown skillet.

"Hey, lady, cut that out and just give me the money or I'll shoot you," though only the landlady verbally understood him.

"What language is that? I'm not close enough yet to understand another person's thoughts."

I think it's Italian. You mean you'll be able to read some other person's mind in time? Never mind that now. I've got to stop that man before someone gets hurt.

+++

Mrs. Mondella, the landlady, spotted Robert, so this time she yelled in broken English, "I no give you nothing. Thief! Ladro! Bastardo! Get outta here."

Robert yelled at the man, "Hey you! Beat it or I'll call the cops!"

The large man turned to face Robert and fired.

Robert fell to the floor as the gunman ran into the hallway and out of the house.

"Oh, Dio Mio no—Mistah Ackers—he been shot!" Mrs. Mondella screamed.

┿┿┿

Minutes later the darkness began to fade, but as light began to return with his vision, it was not any shade of blue that Robert Ackers was expecting to see.

"What hit me? Why didn't you protect me?" he mumbled aloud.

"Oh lay still, mio brave boy," answered a worried voice that wasn't the medallion.

Once fully conscious, Ackers' first reflex was, "OW! My head!" as his hand went to where the bullet grazed his skull.

Mrs. Mondella was bending over Robert's stunned body on the floor. "Don't you move," she pleaded. "I put a damp cloth on you head. You bleed so much when that ladro shoot at you, I thought he kill you. He only hit you— how you a say? Tiny bit on top. You gonna have a big head hurt now but you be fine later. Sorry I could no protect you. You came a rushing in to help me and make that bastardo run out. Thank you."

Looking around and remembering what happened, Robert said, "Oh— right. Are you okay Mrs. Mondella?"

"Sì, I am fine. Thanks to you. Now you rest there while I get a doctor."

I actually got shot? Do I need a doctor?

"*Robert, if your inquiry was directed at me, your head was barely grazed by a projectile from the man's weapon. I have already stopped the bleeding and am starting to heal the wound. It will be completely closed in a day or so. There was a slight injury to your brain, but that is also being healed.*"

Robert thought, *Okay, but why didn't you protect me? You know, put up some kind of force field or something?*

"*Because I cannot do something unless you will it. You did not have time to make such a request in this instance.*"

The sound of a telephone dialing nearby interrupted the medallion's explanation.

"Mrs. Mondella, don't bother calling for a doctor, I'm okay now," Ackers insisted while trying to sit up.

The landlady turned back from the wall-mounted pay phone in the hall to look at Robert, before hanging up. She reentered her apartment and shut the door. Going to the sink, she returned by his side with another damp cloth for his forehead, which had stopped bleeding.

"You should lay down and rest Mistah Ackers. Maybe go see a doctor anyway?"

"I don't think I need to. Just give me a couple of minutes and I should be able to stand. You can see my head has stopped bleeding. I heal quickly Mrs. Mondella. I'll be okay. But I need to know, who *was* that? Do you know him?"

"Sì," she said, wiping her hands on her apron to dry them. "He was a frien' of my late husband, before my Alphonso was killed in his store. Anyway, I thought he was a frien'. So I let him in when he knocked but he was no frien' to me! He came for money he say my Alphonso owe him. That is big lie; my Alphonso never borrow money from nobody."

Standing up, Robert gave the bloody cloth back to Mrs. Mondella. "Well, you should call the police and have him arrested. I hope he doesn't come back. I was on my way to the diner. Do you want me to bring anything back for you?"

"Oh, no. I make dinnah soon. Do you want to stay for it? I make a good spaghetti and meatballs, with a deliziosa tomato sauce. You like that, yes?" She was almost pleading.

"Thank you Mrs. Mondella, but maybe another time. It sounds great, but there's someone I want to meet— Uh, that is, I made arrangements to eat at the diner."

Mrs. Mondella smiled broadly. "Oh. You maybe meet a girl at the diner? I understand now. You go see her then. Thank you again Mistah Ackers. You take care of your head now."

"I will," he said as she escorted him to the door. "You lock up after me too."

Walking down the hall and out of the building, Robert thought, *Boy, that really hurt.*

"*Maybe we should practice some shield projection, so it will come quickly to mind in a similar situation.*"

We'll discuss it further when we get back to the apartment. Right now I'm hungry, Ackers replied.

"*Robert, she offered you a meal in exchange for your help. Why did you not accept it? Is that standard procedure for your landlady?"*

Look, I didn't want her to feel obligated for me helping her out of that situation with the gunman. I wasn't planning on getting shot in the process! She's a nice lady, and also very lonely since her husband was killed.

"Lonely? What is lonely?"

It's an emotion people feel when someone they are used to having around is no longer with them. Most people form pair bonds with other people, like lovers getting married. Sometimes it's just a couple of people forming bonds of friendship. They do things together and spend time together. A person alone, without friends or spouses, might feel lonely. Robert did his best to explain, but it was a jumble of words and feelings. Still the medallion seemed to be able to sort it out.

"I see. I do not entirely understand and cannot express that emotion as you describe it. Yet my instructions do require me to create a bond with a person, which I have done with you. I know that we are not lovers who could marry, as I have seen that in your thoughts about your landlady. Are we friends?"

Frankly, I don't know what we are, Ackers admitted. *It's a most unusual relationship. As you noted humans have formed relationships with animals, as well as with other humans. Having a relationship with an inanimate object is— Well, it's different.*

"You consider me an inanimate object?"

That was uncomfortable ground for Robert. *Technically you are a non-living, non-breathing manufactured item. You don't have the spark of life, at least biologically. On the other hand you think, ask questions, which denotes some sort of curiosity. You do seem to grow in a way, certainly not in a physical sense, but mentally. These are qualities which, at least in part, define life, and therefore do not point to something wholly inanimate. Truthfully you have me stumped. I don't know how to define you,* he conceded. *I know some people seem to think of their cars and other methods of transportation as having personalities. They even give them names and form bonds with them. But those things don't communicate with their owners. You do and uh… Oh, I just don't know!* Ackers was frustrated with the whole concept.

"You do know Robert. I remember part of your description of living organisms included taking in sustenance and excreting waste. Is that not also part of being alive?"

In one sense, yeah. I know your sustenance, catalyzed by me, is from ambient radiation and such. What do you excrete?

A feeling of reticence emanated through him before the medallion responded.

"I would rather not discuss it."

Why not? You said something once about shining excess light. Is that dangerous to humans? To me?

"No. But, do you like discussing your excretions?"

Robert made a wry face and thought, *Not really, but I would like to know more about you, so give me some sort of answer. It'll help build that bond of trust between us.*

A mental feeling of unease overcame Robert, which he equated to the medallion's equivalent of a sigh or unhappy shrug.

"Very well. As you know, I absorb radiation of different types. Sunlight, which includes different wave lengths of energy plus various forms of radiation which come from outer space, which you might call cosmic radiation or something similar. I could not do this initially without being in direct contact with you, although I can absorb it now if I am, say within a few feet, to catalyze this action. My excretions are also in the form of energy or radiation. This type of energy is mostly invisible to and does not affect other life forms, like humans or the various animals and vegetation around us. Sometimes, when I have a problem digesting or absorbing the energy, it may become briefly visible, as a flash in the visible spectrum. Visible to humans. Like a burst or bubble of light."

Like a human passing intestinal gas? Ackers asked, trying not to chuckle.

The medallion took a long pause before saying, *"Yes."*

In other words, you fart! Ackers couldn't suppress his reaction to the idea much longer.

Another mental feeling of... embarrassment?

"Must you be so crude?" his companion asked. *"I would not characterize it that way. Besides, it is quite brief and light has no aspect of smell. You sometimes—"*

Robert began to laugh. *That has to be one of the most human things I've heard from you yet.*

Continuing to laugh out loud, Robert passed some people on the street that looked at him like he was crazy for laughing at nothing.

+++

Still in a humorous mood, after a few minutes of walking along the avenue, they reached the diner.

Entering the busy establishment, Robert looked around and spotted a booth close to the door to sit in.

"Why did you choose to sit here specifically? The medallion questioned in a curious tone. *There are other empty seating spots all around."*

I prefer this booth, was Ackers' curt reply.

An attractive young brunette approached. Her hair fell to her shoulders and its smell reminded Robert of fresh flowers. She wore an apron with a name tag on her blouse that said Sarah.

"Hello Mr. Ackers. Do you need a menu?" she asked.

"No, thank you Sarah, I know what I want and please, call me Robert. I'll have a chicken salad on rye with lettuce and tomatoes. An order of french fries and a soda."

Flashing him a big smile she said, "Okay. I'll be back with your soda in a minute," then turned to walk away. Ackers watched her go with a slight smile on his face. She wrote the order on her pad before tearing the top page off and giving it to the short order cook.

"Your blood pressure went way up and your body had some other reactions just now," observed the medallion, currently sitting in Robert's shirt pocket. *"Are they the result of your proximity to the female?"*

Robert refused to answer as he kept staring at Sarah whenever he could without her being aware of it. Now if he could just find a way to speak to her privately!

CHAPTER 4

At the local police precinct, the desk sergeant looked up from his paperwork and said to a just arriving officer, "After roll call, see the captain. He wants to talk to you."

"Me? Why?" Officer Malcolm McGarry asked.

The desk sergeant simply shrugged his shoulders. "How would I know? Did you do something I don't know about?"

"No, Sarge. Nothing," swore McGarry.

"Well, just do as you're told and hopefully it will all work out."

"Yes Sarge," Officer McGarry replied, while still wondering what might have happened to warrant the attention.

+++

Following orders, the officer soon presented himself to the Captain's secretary.

"Bridgett. Um, the captain wants to see me. Do you know what it's about?"

Bridgett Mahoney, a pert young freckled red head looked up from her paperwork and smiled. "Oh, hi Malcolm. No, I don't know why but just go on in. He's waiting for you."

Walking into Captain Sean Rogen's office, Officer McGarry stood at attention in front of the man seated behind his desk.

"Ah, McGarry. Sit down, please. I just have a few questions for you about this incident report you filed."

"Questions, sir?" the officer asked while complying with the request.

"Yes. About the accident last night and the um, blue light."

"Oh, that," McGarry replied with a frown before sighing in relief. "What do you want to know?"

"Just tell me what happened," requested the Captain. "Start at the beginning and don't leave anything out."

McGarry nodded. "Yes, sir. Well I was close to finishing my beat, ready to return to the precinct when a squad car pulls up and says we need to respond to a call about an accident on Broadway. I jumped onto the running board and we raced to the scene. We'd heard a loud bang as we turned the corner and saw a truck and a car had crashed into each other. They looked like they'd just blown up. There was shattered glass all around, mostly from the vehicles. No other damage I could see then, except the vehicles were still burning and a fire truck was pulling up. An ambulance was already there and the crew was treating three people. A man, a woman, and their child. Their names and address are in the report."

"Yes. Continue," requested Rogen.

"I'm no doctor but they looked to be mostly okay. Maybe just stunned, although the man may have been somewhat burned, but not too badly. They were all starting to come around when we arrived. The truck driver was also there, over to one side. He had a head injury and was bleeding, but didn't look too bad either. The ambulance people were concentrating on treating the family then."

"Okay. I understand everything so far. But what about this blue light?" the Captain asked.

It was all McGarry could do to keep from sighing again, knowing that it would come up and afraid to sound like a total loony. "Well sir, next to the three people was this man shaped... I don't know how to describe it—

him. A blob I guess? It was about seven feet tall, big and pulsing blue, and you could see inside it a darker man shape. The darker shape inside was maybe just under six feet tall. When I asked what happened, a bystander yelled out that the blue light had saved the three people and protected the husband when the car exploded."

"How did he, or it, accomplish that?" Rogen wanted to know. The officer before him raised his hands and shrugged.

"I have no idea sir, and neither did any of the witnesses in the crowd when we questioned them," McGarry replied. "Anyway, when I asked him—it, his name, he just said 'Blue Light' and that he had to go. Then it ran off, faster than I could follow. It turned the corner and by the time I got there— there was nothing."

"I see. What about the truck driver?"

"When I turned around to talk to him he had also disappeared. Couldn't find him. The other officers believe the truck was responsible for the accident, which is why he skedaddled before the ambulance people could treat him or we had a chance to question him."

"I see. Thank you. That will be all officer. You can return to your beat and duties now."

"Yes, sir," McGarry said, standing up and saluting his Captain, before leaving Rogen's office somewhat relieved.

+++

Rogen sat for a few minutes, contemplating what he just heard.

Then he reached over and clicked a switch on his desk intercom. "Bridgett, has Officer O'Hare arrived yet?"

A tinny voice replied, "Yes, sir."

"Please send him in."

Another police officer entered the room, standing in front of the Captain's desk. "You asked to see me sir?"

"Yes, O'Hare. Thank you. It's about this incident report you filed," Rogen said, holding up the appropriate paperwork. "About the couple that was mugged in the alley."

"Yes, sir. Kinda strange that one sir."

"Please tell me about it."

O'Hare shrugged. "Well, it's all in the report sir but I was walking my beat when I heard a bunch of shots. With the echoes between buildings, I heard them clear as day since the street was quiet that late in the evening. It took me a few minutes to reach where they were coming from, since it was a couple of blocks away. I ran to an alley and turned on my flashlight where I see this young couple, Mr. and Mrs. Leventhal, clutching each other against a brick wall, while two men were prone in the alley, unconscious. A pair of guns lay up against another wall. I later discovered both were totally empty, which agreed with all the spent bullets lying on the ground too."

"Did the men shoot the couple, or each other?" Rogen wanted to know.

"No sir," replied O'Hare. "When I spoke with the couple, they said the two men pulled out guns and ordered them into the alley. There they demanded their money and watches, along with the woman's ring and necklace."

"So you didn't stop the robbery?"

"No sir," O'Hare admitted. "I would have if I was there, but–"

"Then who did?" Rogen interrupted.

"It was at this time, according to the couple, there appeared a blue light which momentarily blinded all of them. When they could see again, a weird machine-like voice spoke and told the gunmen to drop their weapons, leave the couple alone, and get out of the alley. The gunmen instead shot at the light until their guns were empty and the blue light's, um, arms expanded in their direction. It slapped away the guns and then knocked them both out."

Rogen said little but just stared at his second witness of the day. O'Hare went on.

"With that it turned to the couple and asked if they were okay and they say it told them not be afraid of— him. Whatever. It said that the police would be there soon and they should tell the officer—that was me sir— what happened."

"And?"

"Well, Mr. Leventhal claims he said to the blue light thing, 'Tell them what happened? That a blue light came in and knocked the two guys out?' Then he claims the blue light said, 'I like that. Yes. Tell them Blue Light did it, and that I'll be around.' Then the blue light ran off, though I never seen it before I entered the alley."

"Is that all O'Hare?" Rogen prompted in a flat tone with no more expression than he would have if he'd just heard about an average robbery.

"It's all they could tell me, sir. They were in a bit of shock and happy they weren't hurt. I got their names and address and they're pressing charges against the muggers. We arrested the men and they're in holding, in separate cells. We also picked up their guns and all the slugs," reported O'Hare.

"The slugs were all there?"

"Yes sir. They were using .38 caliber revolvers and fired all six shots from each gun. We picked up the spent slugs and we're waiting for ballistics to confirm they were fired from those weapons."

"Won't they have trouble matching the spent slugs to the guns? Weren't they flattened by the wall they hit?" Rogen asked. His police scientists were good, but not that good.

"Actually, sir, they didn't touch the wall. The couple said the bullets just stopped within the blue light, like they froze or something. Then the spent slugs just dropped to the ground."

Now *that* was hard to believe! Captain Rogen looked at Officer O'Hare incredulously. "You mean to say, all twelve bullets just stopped inside the blue light?"

"That's how the Leventhals tell it sir, and they're both in agreement. Now, it's obvious something must have happened, but we haven't figured out exactly what yet," said O'Hare, trying to sound skeptical. "The slugs were in perfect shape. Except for being fired, you'd swear those bullets looked like they just came fresh from the box. Not mashed like they would have been if they'd bounced off the walls, and nothing stuck to them. All were lying on the ground."

"When you came to the scene, this Blue Light was gone?"

"Yes, sir, like I said sir. No sign of him."

Rogen sat back in his chair, still staring blankly at Officer O'Hare. Finally deciding there was nothing else to ask, the Captain said, "Thank you O'Hare. You may return to your post now."

"Yes sir," replied the officer, saluting before leaving.

+++

Within his closed office, Captain Rogen went over the reports again. The attempted mugging ended roughly ten minutes before the car crash, provided the cited incident times were accurate.

He rose from his chair and walked over to a wall map of the precinct. Rogen located the alley and then traced the shortest route to the location of the crash.

He stared at the map, lost in thought before making a decision. Walking back to his desk, Rogen collected the incident reports before reaching for the intercom. "Bridgett, tell my driver to be ready for me in five minutes. Then call the Commissioner's office and tell them I'm on my way with a possible situation."

"Yes Captain," his secretary replied.

+++

As it turned out, the commissioner did not seem concerned about a 'local issue'.

"Handle it on your end and keep me informed," was the indifferent answer before Rogen was dismissed and the preoccupied man went on with his day.

+++

In another part of town sat a rundown brownstone near an elevated track, where commuter trains noisily ran overhead as a stream of cars passed each other on a wide boulevard.

The rear room of one unit looked out on a small, unlit backyard. Inside a short man about thirty-five, dark hair; with dark suit, shirt and tie, looked up as a gunsel entered. The other man already inside with him stayed near the door.

"Clancy, what happened?" the man in the dark suit asked.

"The two mugs you sent to rough up Leventhal got knocked out and arrested. The cops are holding them in the precinct downtown. They'll be taken to court later."

"Just how did they get arrested?" the first man asked.

"I don't know," Clancy admitted. "The story I got is kinda muddled and well, um, pretty fantastic," he added. "It has something to do with a light of some kind."

"A light?" The dark suited man gave his underling a searching look. "What kind of light? How could a light stop two guys who know their business?"

Clancy put up his hands and shook his head. "Boss, I just don't know. I couldn't get any details, and we can't get a shyster in there to brief 'em until later."

"I see. What about the other thing. The delivery?"

"Yeah, about that." Clancy was starting to sweat. This wasn't going well, as he knew it wouldn't. "The truck got into an accident. The car it hit blew up. Everything in the truck burned up with that."

"WHAT!" screamed the Boss. "There was over forty grand worth of stuff in that truck. Where's the driver?"

"He managed to get away, a little groggy from the accident. Hit his head. But we got him before he could take it on the lam and hide away from us. He's in the other room," said Clancy, hoping to save some face.

"Well, bring him in here. NOW!"

"Right away," Clancy turned and nodded to the other hood behind him. The quiet man opened the door and waved. Two other men soon entered, each holding a third by an arm and pushing him forward.

"S-s-s-sir, p-please," he stuttered. "I-I can explain!"

"You was driving the truck, right?" the Boss asked.

"Y-y-yes sir. But the other car raced into the intersection and I didn't have time to stop. The accident's not my fault. It's really not," he pleaded, almost whimpering.

"I see," the Boss said sweetly. "Well, these things happen. So tell me what went on after the crash. Did you see something?"

"Y-y-yes," began the driver. "But... well. I took a hard knock on the head, and what I saw was kinda incredible. I mean, it just seemed so... impossible."

The local mob leader removed the cigar from his hand and rolled it around in his fingers. "Go on."

"I, um— There was this blue light, shaped like a large guy—huge. He runs over to the smashed car and it has started to boin, the car that is, and the blue light thing rams his tentacles or arms or whatever they were through the passenger side windows and drags out the goil and the kid, and moves them to a building. I mean he—it—hoists them like they weighed nuttin' at all."

"Are you serious?" the Boss asked and he said it slowly with plenty of emphasis.

"Y-y-yeah," swore the man. "I seen it, I did! Then he goes to the driver side and, it looked like one tentacle or arm shifts into like dis big door jimmy. He jams it into the side of the door and forces it wider, then the tentacle arm changes again into a hand and he drags the door open. He grabs the big guy and starts to go to where he put the dame and the kid, but the car blows before he gets there. The blast blew him to the ground and the light went dimmer as the fire spread to the truck too. Then the light got bluer as it lit back up again and the blue light thing gets up and placed the guy by the goil and kid. I never seen nuttin' like it before."

"A blue light did all that?"

"I'm pretty sure, yeah. It was shaped like a big man," the truck driver said again, sounding desperate. "It was dis blue light, man shaped. Big and bright thing."

"Hey, Boss," said the thug on the right still holding onto the driver. "For what it's worth, I gabbed with someone else who saw the whole thing. He kinda said the same thing, and I know these two never met," he added, nodding to the driver. "I wouldn't of believed it, but a lot of people in that crowd were saying basically da same thing."

"A blue light. Right. I'll get to that in a minute," promised the Boss, before turning to face the terrified driver. "Now as to you–"

"B-b-b-boss, it weren't my fault. That car just rushed into the road in front of me. I couldn't stop in time to avoid it. I COULDN'T STOP!" he yelled.

"You couldn't stop. Couldn't avoid all that attention we don't need." The Boss turned to the man on the right holding him. "He couldn't stop for the car. What should I do about that, huh, Mike? What do you think I should I do?"

"I dunno, Boss. It's not my place to say. I mean, accidents happen all da time."

"I respect your position," the Boss told Mike, "but this accident cost me forty grand. FORTY GRAND!" he shouted.

Then he turned to face the driver and pointed the cigar at him. "How are you gonna pay me back?"

"I-I-I-I ain't got that kind of dough. I got a wife and two kids to support, but I'll do anything to make up fer it," promised the driver.

The Boss angrily pulled open the top drawer of his desk, grabbed the gun sitting in the open drawer, and shot the petrified man point blank between the eyes. The two men holding him never had a chance to duck.

"You don't got no wife and two kids. Yah got a widow and two orphans is what yah got."

The startled Mike and his partner, still holding onto the other arm of the now lifeless man, looked at their leader.

"What do ya want we should do wit him now, Boss?" Mike asked.

"The usual. Make sure he ain't found. Now get out, all of ya!"

When the door closed and he was all alone, the Boss chomped angrily on what was left of his cigar. "A blue light," he says to himself. "And supposedly a blue light saved Leventhal too. That ain't no coincidence. What are you Mr. Blue Light? Maybe I should call in some reinforcements."

CHAPTER 5

Things with Sarah did not quite go the way he hoped, for he still couldn't work up the nerve to ask her out. So Robert Ackers was back at work writing, finishing up a new story the next morning.

"How are you doing today Robert?" the medallion asked.

Okay. Almost done with this story, he silently replied.

"The topic on this one is a different… What did you call it? Genre?"

Genre is correct. I'm trying to write a mystery this time. What do you think of it?

"I really wasn't paying attention to your writing today, except to note that it was not as… fantastical, like most of your other writing has been. I think you called the other stories Scientifiction?"

Science Fiction, Robert corrected his companion. *I'm trying out different genres to widen my writing markets. The more magazines I have to sell stories to, the wider my audience and the more chances I have to make an honest living.*

"What is next?"

Robert thought about that for a moment before answering, *I've already gone through most of the text and edited it to my satisfaction. Now I mail it to the publisher. Then, I start writing another story.*

"How do you manage to keep track of all your stories?"

I do the best I can, he answered, half distracted while addressing a large envelope. After inserting the manuscript and a cover letter, he sealed the envelope and said, *I need to mail this. Let's go to the post office and then the diner.*

"Is that the only place where you can get food?"

No, but I like eating there. The post office comes first though, Ackers replied with some evasiveness, staring at the medallion sitting next to his typewriter. It was asking a lot of nosy questions all of a sudden.

"So you are going out to send this now?"

Yes! Ackers was getting irritated. *After that I'm going to get something to eat. What's with all the probing questions?*

"It is how I learn about you so I can help you more efficiently. I ask to understand if you are truly in need to go somewhere and why. Or why you prefer this diner where you must pay for food when your landlady would feed you for free. Is the sustenance that superior there? Or, are you going for

Science Fiction, Robert corrected his companion.

another reason?"

What other reason would I have? Ackers snapped mentally.

"*That female servitor, Sarah. Every time you see her you seem to become nervous and a little agitated. Also somewhat—*" The medallion was searching for a term that covered the physical reactions.

Robert Ackers knew where that was going and interrupted the thought conversation. *Look, you need to stop monitoring my condition when I'm not in any danger.*

"*But that response seems indicative of some unsafe event. Was it something about the quality of the meal or–*"

It's not unsafe, I'm just nervous. It's a social situation and I'm not good at them. Some of them can be— uncertain.

"*Uncertain? How? While my experiences are limited to just my interactions with you, last night seemed to be within acceptable norms.*"

Ackers sighed audibly.

Unlike your ability to see into my mind, I can't read hers—not even partially—or any other mind for that matter. Robert reminded the medallion. *I like Sarah and want to get to know her better. But I don't know if she likes me or would be willing to go out with me if I ever find the courage to ask her. That's part of what we call dating. It's how humans of the opposite sex meet and perhaps form a bond.*

"*If you want, I can try to pick up her thoughts on the matter. I might be able to—*"

Robert quickly shouted out, "NO!" Then he reinforced it with a thought. *Never do that.*

"*I do not understand. Do you not want to know how she responds to you?*"

Yes, but not that way. Oh, how do I explain this? He asked himself. *Part of what makes us human is how we communicate, and yes I do want to know how she feels about me. Yet it would be an intrusion into her privacy if I could read her mind, or if I allowed you to do it.*

"*Do not humans also communicate in nonverbal ways?*"

Sighing, Robert thought, *Of course we do, but it's up to us to figure out what signals the other person is sending by their posture, facial features, and other gestures. Without you, I'm not at all telepathic and that would be cheating since she couldn't do the same with me.*

"*I am not sure I understand, but will accept this for now if it makes you more comfortable. However, I am supposed to protect and guide you. This is at odds with the way you and I communicate if I cannot know about all conditions that affect you.*"

Ackers had to concede that. *I understand what you're telling me, but you're not human like me or Sarah. This is the only way you and I can share information quickly. That's vital in a dangerous situation, but not for regular human-to-human interaction. Please stop interfering in my social life.*

"*I will do as you ask, but you must allow me to monitor conditions around you. If it would be easier, I could form a tendril and write down all of our communications. Or, I could form a speaker and send sound waves to you as a voice. I do somewhat like that idea.*"

Robert was surprised to hear those possibilities and so he filed that away in his mind as he readied himself to go out. He reached for the medallion and tucked it into a pocket. *Those are interesting suggestions that we might use sometime, but not in public. This way of communicating is quicker for us and I don't want others seeing or hearing you. I need to keep you a secret.*

"*I must inquire. Why that is important?*"

It gives me a hidden advantage. What others don't know they can't use against me or defend themselves against either of us. And some people may think I'm crazy—mentally unstable—if they saw me talking to myself. That could become a very big problem.

"*I will defer to your judgment in this case, but I may not always do so if I find it necessary.*"

Fair enough. Ackers was at the door, his manuscript in hand, and fumbling for his keys. *It's time to get going.*

Will this post office still be available for your purpose?"

The local branch is open till five. It's only 2:30 PM now and not far away, but I hope there isn't much of a line. I need postage stamps too. If it's too busy I'll just buy the stamps. I can put them on myself and mail this at the local drop box, Ackers added as he locked his apartment door behind him before heading downstairs.

+++

The day was cool and cloudy. Only a few people were currently using the sidewalk. Traffic was light on the street, with cars passing in both directions, and even a horse drawn cart. A street vendor selling fruits and vegetables from a push cart was hawking his wares on the corner. The medallion was in one of Ackers' front pants pockets but quiet, so he figured it was doing as suggested, trying to take everything in silently. He took a deep breath of air and tensed and relaxed muscles in his neck and shoulders that were knotted up from hunching over the typewriter. As much as he enjoyed writing when it went well, it was good to get out for a while.

Turning the corner, Robert heard screams and shouts, as people were streaming out of the local bank.

Something's not right. Let's take a closer look, he suggested, not waiting for a response.

Maneuvering around the crowd rushing out, Ackers peered into the big plate glass window and saw three men wearing masks. The trio were all pointing guns at the cashier windows while another masked man was walking behind the counter, filling a bag with cash from the tellers' individual drawers.

It's a robbery! In broad daylight no less. How's your energy level?

"I am almost fully charged. What do you intend to do?"

I think it's time for Blue Light to make an appearance. Anyone looking this way?

"They are all running away, with no one looking in your direction."

Okay, light me up.

Immediately the blue light construct surrounded him. Ackers moved through the doors, attracting amazed stares from the cashiers. The bag man behind the counter looked up in stunned disbelief before motioning to his companions and pulling his own weapon.

Being a regular customer, Robert was familiar with the bank layout. In front was the cashier counter with cages for each teller. To the left were desks for the various clerks. Behind them offices for the bank officials, with every door currently closed. To the right were the standing tables with forms for the customers and a day/date holder. Some remodeling work was being done near the window, for some loose lumber laid on the floor as well as a sledgehammer for breaking some of the floor tiles. The area was roped off, the crew must have left for the day.

The bag man pointed his revolver at the large blue shape. "Shoot him. Take him down boys!" he yelled as the trio started firing.

Create a shield and deflect the bullets. Make sure no one is standing in the direction of the deflection.

Before the shots reached him, Blue Light projected an angled shield, deflecting the bullets to one side. But, having a different angle, the gunman behind the counter fired and it hit in a less protected spot.

Ow! What happened?

"Not foreseeing an immediate need in that area, I decreased the protection on that side when I created the shield. You are bleeding."

Ackers looked down in shock. *Not badly. The protection slowed the slug down a lot, but it got through and nicked me in the arm. Strengthen the shield in that direction,* he ordered, to which his companion complied.

With so much going on, it was hard to keep track of everything. Focusing his attention back on the robbers, Ackers said, *One gunner has run out of ammo for now. Where are the other two?*

"One is moving to the door. The man behind the counter is heading for the exit in back. I cannot account for the third yet."

Can you create a wall for that guy in back and prevent him from getting out that way without weakening the shield, while I take care of these guys?

"Yes, I am doing that now." The Blue Light projected out toward the back of the bank as Ackers began to move toward the other gunmen. "What are your intentions?"

I'm going to push the shield in their direction and slam them against that counter. For the guy on my right, before he reloads his gun, extend an arm and slap him down.

"Where is he? He moved."

That wasn't good! *Did he run out the door?* There was the sound of sirens wailing in the distance but drawing closer. Somebody had called the police.

"I did not see him do so. I am doing too many things at once to do a thermal scan of the area—"

The medallion was interrupted as Ackers felt a sudden, somewhat numbing impact from behind. He stumbled forward and almost fell.

The missing gunman had picked up the construction sledgehammer and struck him in the back! The shield was not strong there and so Ackers staggered and almost blacked out.

"Robert you must remain conscious and stay on your feet!" the medallion shouted in his mind, while Ackers tried to work his way through the pain of the blow and concentrate on controlling the situation before one of the innocent cashiers got hurt. His assailant was setting up for another swing when a large blue arm swept back with great force and flung the masked man across the floor. Landing close to the entrance with a thump, the slightly stunned robber dropped the sledgehammer and played dead.

Trapped behind the counter, the bag man aimed his revolver at Blue Light, who lost track of the robber behind him by the door. He escaped as the others struggled.

Blue Light had just wrestled the bag man's weapon away when police officers finally rushed into the bank, weapons drawn.

Seeing the police and realizing he was outnumbered with no possible escape, the would-be robber dropped the bag of loot and raised his hands in surrender.

"Police—freeze!" The sergeant commanded as his men fanned out through the bank. "Hands up all of–"

He stopped dead in mid-sentence upon seeing the large and glowing man shape holding the two men against the cashier counter and cautiously walked over to Blue Light.

"What the heck are you? Um— raise your— hands sir."

From the blue mass, the flat mechanical voice said, "I am Blue Light. I saw the robbery in progress and came in to assist. One man escaped, just before you got here. I will release these two for you to cuff. I'm sure some of the people in here will be glad to tell you what they saw."

With that he turned and started for the door.

The police sergeant who had approached him yelled out, "Hey, you can't leave yet. We need to question you. Boys, don't let that uh— that big blue man out yet."

A couple of officers started to approach as Blue Light stopped in place. "Sergeant, I do not want a confrontation with the police. I have stopped the robbery for you. One criminal got away. There is nothing else I can accomplish here. So I am leaving now."

The policemen seemed uncertain, but they didn't move. Their sergeant approached carefully, but his voice was grim and determined. "We appreciate that, but until we get this sorted out, you're not going anywhere." He still had his weapon drawn. It was a tense standoff moment.

"Robert, they are all armed and dangerous. Should I just move them out of the way or take more drastic action?" the medallion asked.

Neither. I don't want to fight the police. They're the good guys here and just doing their job enforcing the law. There must be another way to get past them without hurting them.

"How about if I refract light instead of projecting it?"

Refract light— Oh do you mean we would become invisible? It was a science fiction term he was familiar with.

"Not truly invisible. They would still see the objects around and behind us, but they would not see us. We could then move past them as well as the officers at the door. Would that be useful?"

Yes, but answer this first. Wouldn't I then be unable to see too?

"Yes, but I can lead us out easily enough with an invisible signal. Similar to what your terrestrial bats do with echo location, but without an audible sound."

One other thing. We're kind of big in this form. Can you reduce the size of the body around me? I don't think we need to worry about shielding if they can't see me. Just keep enough mass to surround me with that refraction field, and it would be easier to move past the cops by the door.

"*Yes, I can do that.*"

Great. Do it now!

+++

Suddenly, he was gone. Officers, handcuffed criminals, and bank employees straggling out of hiding stared at where Blue Light had been a moment before.

The police began searching the bank but couldn't find any trace of the big blue form.

While they were frantically hunting for him, one of the front doors opened and then shut as if by magic, with no one appearing to go out or come in.

CHAPTER 6

The lone crook who had managed to escape out the front door while the big blue thing was distracted by the gun fire ran to a nearby alley and took refuge there. He waited, in case any of his fellow gunmen managed to escape. The police sirens told a different story, which made him stay in place until it was safe to attempt fleeing.

After several minutes the man took the risk of peering around the corner. The only indication of police were their cars still parked outside. He was about to turn and leave when the bank door opened, but nothing came out.

With that he started running to the other end of the alley and climbed over the wooden slat fence to freedom.

+++

Inside the bank, the police finished cuffing the robbers and were taking witness statements when one officer noticed a large manila envelope on the floor near the lumber. He recognized its destination as one of his favorite pulp magazine publishers, but it also bore a local return address for a Robert Ackers.

"Sarge, I found this on the floor near that window, by the lumber over there," he explained, turning it over to his superior.

"Thanks," said the Sergeant, staring at the mail. "Might have been dropped by a bank customer fleeing as the robbery began. Take this crew back to the precinct and book them while I report to Captain Rogen. I'll see what he thinks of this. Maybe this guy saw something we can use. Too many of these robberies lately."

+++

A few minutes after arriving at the precinct, the Sergeant was in his Captain's office.

"Cap'n Rogen, just back from the bank job, and you'll get a full report once I have a chance to write it up. But I thought you'd want to know now that the Blue Light guy showed up again."

That perked up the Captain's ears, and he sat forward in his desk chair. "I want to hear every detail, especially about the Blue Light," Rogen ordered. "Come in and shut the door."

The Sergeant immediately complied and stood before his superior with arms at his side. "We were notified there was a robbery in progress at the bank a few blocks away," he began. "With several officers in a couple of cars, we went in. As far as we can figure there were four thugs involved. All the customers had been allowed to leave, the bank brass had locked themselves in their offices, but three cashiers had been held at gunpoint until— Well, until the Blue Light guy came in. Things must have gotten pretty intense; the girls were already rattled and ducked down screaming when the shooting started, so their accounts vary a little bit. Sounds like the hoodlums had heard of this Blue Light guy and were emptying their cylinders into him, but he didn't fall or even flinch. The rest is kinda sketchy, but when we got there one of Blue Light's... I guess you'd call it an arm—" he seemed uncertain. "Well it was pressing two men against the counter so they couldn't move.

"Here's where it gets really strange," the Sergeant warned his superior. "A third one of those crooks was in back of the cashier's counter, he'd been banging on the rear exit door, which was blocked by another one of Blue Light's... arms. Those are some real long arms that guy has! When he noticed us, Blue Light let 'em all go and said to cuff 'em, and he warned us that a fourth man had run out before we got there."

Rogen was stunned. "So the Blue Light... this giant glowing man, he was holding the crooks with two arms that were different lengths so that one could reach to the back exit?" When the Sergeant nodded sheepishly and shrugged, Rogen waved his hands a bit indicating he'd accept that— for now. "Then what happened?"

"It gets stranger. We had enough men in there with the backups arriving to take out the crooks, so we surrounded the Blue Light and I told him he had to come in for questioning. He just stood there for a bit, and then it was like—" He had to find a way to explain it. "It was like somebody pulled the chain or clicked the switch. He just vanished."

Rogen almost came to his feet. "You're telling me that an eight foot blue glowing guy with six foot arms—I know because I've been in that bank enough times—just disappeared before your eyes." At the uncomfortable nod he got, Rogen sat back in his chair.

"Cap'n, it's the God's honest truth, I swear," the thoroughly abashed Sergeant said. With the report was finished, the Captain just sat there and stared at his underling in disbelief.

"You know, if anybody else came in here and told me that besides every other completely impossible thing this Blue Light guy accomplishes, he also turns invisible, I would have put him on medical leave. But I know you too well."

"Sir, the other cops will tell you the same thing," was the Sergeant's only response.

"That at one point his arms were two different shapes and lengths as well?"

He got a lopsided smile. "Well, ah, that is Sir, when this Blue Light released the men, his arms sort of, um, retracted into his— its— body and became regular looking arms again."

Rogen gaped at the Sergeant with new astonishment.

"So the Blue Light… this thing changes its shape at will. Then he turned invisible. Is that what you're saying?"

The Sergeant's face flushed as he shrugged. "Yes sir."

"And both this Blue Light and one suspect escaped?"

"The witnesses, including this Blue Light character, all swear there were four robbers at the start but we only arrested three."

Rogen remained silent, staring into space.

The Sergeant was fearful the Captain might think he was insane or had just concocted the story with the other responding officers because of the missing criminal, but even he knew that fantastic Blue Light stories were beginning to pop up all over. When Rogen finally spoke again, all he said was, "Anything else?"

"Oh yeah. One of the men found this at the scene," said the Sergeant, as he pulled something out of his shirt and handed it to Rogen. It was the manila envelope. "We found this in the bank. Thought maybe we should return it to the guy looking to mail it."

The Captain examined the package, recognizing the name from an earlier report before saying, "I see. Thank you. You're dismissed Sergeant. Oh, and tell the desk to invite this," looking at the manila envelope, "Robert Ackers to come see me to retrieve this. Soon."

"Yes, sir."

Alone in the office after the Sergeant left, Rogen laid the envelope on his desk and stared at it, lost in thought. *So who are you Robert Ackers? Innocent bystander or something else?*

+++

After walking invisibly a couple of blocks away from the bank, Robert Ackers ducked into an alley for a moment.

Okay. You can turn the field off now, he told the medallion.

Able to see on his own again, the first thing Robert did was to examine his arms. Where the bullet ripped his sleeve was obvious, but it was only a crease in the skin. Thankfully it had not bled much, and where the shot scraped bare flesh appeared healed.

This quick healing is your work? He asked the medallion.

"*Of course. One of my primary responsibilities is your health and safety.*"

Thanks. You know, it's good to be able to see normally again. It was kind of weird going someplace and not seeing where we were.

"*Comparable to being in the dark without a light to guide you, if you did not have me.*"

Exactly. Now then, I still need to go to the post office and give them...

He didn't have the manila envelope with the manuscript! He searched himself repeatedly before checking the ground around his feet.

The package with my story. It's gone!

"*You dropped it inside the building, just before I turned on the blue light construct.*"

You saw that and didn't tell me?

"*You could not afford to be distracted at the time. There was too much to do to subdue those 'crooks' as you referred to them, and then the police came in and that also made you tense. I did not want to delay you any further. At the time you were only interested in getting away unseen.*"

Ackers was upset to lose that copy of the story, but he had no idea what he could do about it under the circumstances. *Well, I can't go back for it now. Besides all those police being still there, it's after three and the bank will be closed anyway,* he realized, glancing at his wristwatch with a sigh. A look of resignation crossed Robert's face. *I'll go back to the bank tomorrow morning and ask for it. It'll just get mailed out a day late. I'm hungry now anyway, might as well get something to eat. Let's go to the diner.*

"*Are you sure you do not want to go back to your living quarters and get some rest instead? As before, a number of your body signs are elevated and have not yet returned to their base levels.*"

No, I'm hungry. I'm sure I'll calm down while sitting in the diner.

"*In the same booth, with the same female attending you? I believe it is more accurate to say her close presence would make you feel less agitated about the incident in the bank,*" the medallion suggested.

Robert smiled sheepishly. *Yeah, that too,* he admitted.

+++

A few minutes later, Robert entered the diner and saw that his preferred booth was empty. The medallion had remained silent during the entire walk but now he felt a sense of certainty coming from it as he slid into place.

While she waved upon seeing him, the diner was busy, so it was a few minutes before Sarah walked over. "Hi Mister... Robert," she said with a smile. "How are you today?"

"I'm okay Sarah, but very hungry."

"Well, you came to the right place. What can I get you, or would you prefer to look at the menu first?"

Robert asked, "What's the blue plate special today?"

"Well, we have a meatloaf with mashed potatoes and green beans. We also have a grilled salmon with baked potato and spinach. And we also—"

Robert interjected. "No, the salmon is perfect. I'll have a soda with that, but some water to start."

Writing on her order pad, Sarah smiled at him again. "Okay Robert. It'll take a few minutes. Do you want butter or sour cream with the potato?"

"Butter, thanks."

"Gotcha. I'll go get your water and soda," she said, before walking away with a flourish.

"*Robert, considering what I am sensing from you right now and the way you are staring, is there something wrong with her?"* the medallion in his pants pocket asked.

Ackers turned his attention back to face the table surface and mentally sighed. *No. Absolutely nothing is wrong with Sarah. It's just the way she walks is... attention grabbing.*

"I see how your body is reacting. Some of your organic chemicals are—"

I know, I know, he interrupted. *They're elevating. That's normal.*

"Highly elevated in some instances," confirmed the medallion.

Robert shook his head. *Look, I really wish you'd stop monitoring that here. It's just a way men can react to an attractive girl. And that isn't considered a dangerous situation—well not in most cases.*

"This is somewhat confusing Robert. I assume this is some sort of mating ritual? I cannot comprehend the procedures, let alone the rules of engagement, if I cannot monitor them."

Robert smiled. *Well, how would you handle it if I monitored your mating rituals?*

"How could you do that? I do not have mating rituals in my programming. I do not even understand the question," admitted the medallion.

You don't mate? It was more a tease than a valid question.

"I do not believe so... That is, I have no protocol for it... I have never experienced a need for it—"

Have you ever met another medallion like you? The impression the medallion gave him was one of confusion tinged with concern about inadequacy.

"These are some interesting questions you ask Robert and I will research them later. I do not remember coming into proximity to another like me, nor do I know if any others exist. Even if I did, I have no idea what the... mating ritual of such an artificial interface would be like. Provided there even is one. That is the only answer I can provide at this time."

Ackers let it go as Sarah came back over with his drinks. "Here you are Robert. The food will be ready soon. Can I get you some rolls and butter in the meantime?"

He looked up at her and smiled. "Sure, Sarah. Thank you." He still watched her with a sigh as she walked away.

"There it is again. That spike in—"

Yes, I know, now stop it, he thought with another sigh. *Say, we haven't chosen a name for you. Do you have one?* Robert asked, wanting to change the subject.

"A designation? I do not know. I have never considered it before, nor do I

find anything in my available data stores."

Well, I think it would actually make our... talks, go easier if you had a name. Let's see, you're a blue medallion, but Medallion is too long and I don't feel like calling you Blue. How about Med? It'll be short for medallion. What do you think?

"I have no preference, so that is satisfactory. Med is now my designation unless I find out I have a designation already."

Now that we've got that sorted out, we need to discuss another item. In the bank we lost sight of the fourth guy. He slammed me with that sledgehammer and that hurt like heck. If it was a gun, he might have seriously injured or even killed me. We need to come up with a strategy for protecting all sides of me.

"What sort of strategy are you suggesting?"

Well Med, there should be some way to monitor the entire area around us so we never lose track of where people are. That way they can't surprise us.

"I understand Robert," Med said, before pausing to contemplate the problem. It was a good five seconds, according to the clock on the diner wall, before his companion 'spoke' again. "You know how I can project a monitor inside the blue light shell which shows you my power level?"

Yes. But I can only look at so many things at once while I'm trying to fight.

"Understood. Your brain's processing speed is slow compared to me and it also runs your senses as well as your other body functions. Perhaps I could create one with a 360 degree view of the surrounding area. It would appear as sort of a map around you in a display, generated from my location signal. I could keep watch with that while you do other things."

Will that distract you from any other commands I might give you?

"Unlike you humans, I can partition my processing unit into different functions which do not require constant attention from my core. As with the power display, it will take only a small portion of my total unit capability and will not significantly reduce my response time."

Just then Sarah walked over with a couple of plates and placed them in front of Ackers. He had been so deep into the conversation with Med, he flinched a little when she spoke. "Here you go Robert. Do you need anything else?" she asked with a smile.

He shook his head to cover the involuntary movement. "I'll call on you if I do. Thanks Sarah." As she turned away he said, "Um…" and she stopped to look back.

"Do not hesitate this time Robert," Med urged.

"Say— w-what time to you get off work?" he managed to ask without too much stuttering.

Sarah smiled at him warmly. "About seven. Why?" Her smile said she knew what was coming, but Ackers shifted uncomfortably in his seat, looked down at the food, and then back up at her.

"Uh, well, I wanted to know— um— because—"

"Say it Robert."

Shut up Med—this is tough enough without a coach! Sarah was still smiling and trying to be patient, but she had to get going. The diner was getting busy now.

"Look… um, if you're okay with it, I thought we could go get some coffee later. Not here, obviously."

Sarah's smile grew broader and her eyes crinkled, making him feel like he'd just won a very important uphill battle. "I'd like that Robert. I'd like that a lot. Meet me here at seven?"

Robert Ackers felt a combination of relief and shock, but he shakily returned the big smile with one of his own and nodded. "Sure, definitely."

"Good! See you then," Sarah said and walked away. With a feeling of triumph, Robert turned his attention toward his food, eating ravenously while exuding a happiness even Med's highly advanced capabilities were unnecessary to detect.

"Robert, you are experiencing something I do not understand. You have those same elevated chemicals as before, and your heart is beating fast, but you seem less apprehensive and more confident. What changed your mood?"

I guess I'd call it joy or elation. There was some uncertainty before I got up the nerve to ask her out, but when she said yes, I was thrilled.

"Elation and joy, thrill and uncertainty. These are all human reactions to mating rituals?"

When things go well, yes. We get these feelings.

"How do you sense these feelings?"

Robert was in a good mood to answer now. He slowed his chewing and thought about it, because Med needed to be able to differentiate between different types of human awareness. *Feelings are emotions, sensations that are part of our unconscious reactions. They generally don't include any thought, they just happen. Animals and people experience them. You can see them in dogs—those are domesticated canines—by the way they act. Wagging their tail and jumping on you when you come home after being away. Cats are domestic felines, and they also have their ways of expressing their feelings. They purr and like to sit with you.*

Humans can feel these sensations at various times depending on what's going on around them. For example, at the car explosion and in the bank, I felt some fear. Here I felt uneasy at first and then happy that Sarah said yes. I don't know how to describe it any further. Maybe I'll look it up in a dictionary for both of us. You're an intelligent machine of some kind Med. I don't know if you're capable of emotions. Are you?

There was a pause, as if the medallion was thinking it over.

"I find myself unable to completely answer that question," Med finally admitted. "I do know that when you feel something I also have a corresponding reaction, but I cannot put a name to it. Whether or not my responses correlate to yours, I cannot find anything in my core memories to assist in further quantifying this."

Well Med, I'll leave you to figure it out. I'm finished with my meal and want to go home and change.

"Change into what? Are you capable of changing your shape as I can? I did not realize you could do that."

Robert stifled a laugh. *No. Change my clothes for my date. First I need to pay for my food, say goodbye to Sarah, then go back to my apartment.*

"Say goodbye? But she just agreed to see you again later. Are you not going to come back?"

You better believe it Med. You still have a lot to learn about courtesy and consideration, but you're doing pretty well. It's just good manners to say goodbye until you meet again.

+++

If Robert Ackers had not been so distracted by his impending date with Sarah and his silent conversation with Med, he might have noticed the two men sitting in the back booth who were drinking coffee and looking around speculatively. They were dressed in workman's clothing, one with a flat cap, the other a walker in tweed that had seen better days. They'd been there for quite a while and talked in low voices. Flat cap kept eyeing the kitchen and storeroom at the back of the diner.

"Whadya think Mooch? We hit 'em after closing? Been a busy day here," Tweed Walker hat said as the register dinged and the cashier handed Ackers his change and thanked him for coming in again. The other man shot a sideways glance over at the cashier counter and fiddled with his cup. The coffee was cold, but that didn't matter.

"Yeah fer sure Sid, we can do that," he said in a nasal New England drawl. "Let's hit the streets for now, before they get suspicious. That nosy waitress is gonna come ask us do we want pie or sumptin again if we don't move out." He thrust a hand into a pocket of his overalls and fished out a dime for both coffees. "Leave the old bat a li'l tip Sid. We'll get it all back later and then some."

Sid grunted and flipped a coin down to land next to the dime and they sauntered out together. Like a vulture sighting a dead squirrel on the side of the road, the older waitress swept over to their booth to collect her money, clicking her tongue over the half cups of scummy cold coffee and the measly tip. They tied up the booth half the afternoon so that no paying customer could sit there and eat, and all she got was a nickel for herself. When she picked them up, the cups smelled of booze, so they'd had a back pocket pint with them as well. Manager would want to know that. She shook her head over the stogie ashes that had been butted on one saucer, some of it landing on the checkered tablecloth. That would have to be cleaned too.

Creeps and skinflints, that's all she ever got! Oh if she was only as young and pretty as Sarah. Then maybe she could make a decent living as a waitress. It was disheartening, being on her feet all day, and then going home dog-tired to a third floor walk-up, too exhausted to eat, and still be basically broke.

CHAPTER 7

Robert started walking up the tenement stairs to his apartment when the landlady stepped out of her first floor rooms and called to him.

"Mistah Ackers. Dere was a man here to see you," she announced in her broken English, catching him before Robert got too far up the steps.

"A man Mrs. Mondella?" he asked her with just a bit of uneasiness in his voice. "Did he say what he wanted?"

"No. He come and knock on you door. After a few minutes he come back down and speak to me, and he leave me dis," she explained, handing him a small envelope.

"Thank you Mrs. Mondella," Robert said, looking at the plain white envelope with just his name on it. Then he thought to ask, "Are you okay? That other man hasn't come back to bother you, has he?"

"No, thank you Mistah Ackers. I think you chase him away. You wanna come for dinnah?" She looked hopeful.

"No thank you, I just ate. I'll be going out again soon anyway."

Mrs Mondella smiled. "So, does this mean you finally ask out dat girl you so sweet on? Is dat who you're gonna see?"

"Um, yeah I did," replied Robert, trying not to blush. "We're going for coffee later."

"Datsa good thing. Bring her by sometime. I'll give you both a nice dinnah."

Robert's face flushed as he stuttered, "Well, uh, we're not, that is, uh, at that stage yet, Mrs. Mondella."

"Well you have a good time," she said, before going back into her apartment. Ackers felt a little sad telling the kindhearted elder lady no so often, but he needed time alone with Sarah first. Mrs. Mondella was a sweet person, but she was kind of pushy.

"What is in the missive, Robert?" Med asked, trying to get his human companion's mind back on important matters now that they were alone in the entryway.

Wait till we get in the apartment, then I'll open it.

He hustled upstairs and unlocked his apartment, relocking it again on the inside before opening the envelope.

The message within was simple and read: Mr. Ackers, please come to the local precinct house and see Captain Rogen at your first opportunity.

"Robert, what is a precinct house?" Med asked.

That wouldn't have been my first question, but it's a police station, a gathering place for law enforcement officers when they're not out on patrol.

"And who is Captain Rogen?"

Robert looked at the page contemplatively. *I assume he's the local police captain. The leader of the precinct.*

"The leader of the police wants to see you? Why?"

Robert huffed. *That would have been my first question, but I have no idea Med. We'll only find out when we see him. Tomorrow. I have other things to do tonight.*

"Are you still going out on a date with Sarah this evening?"

Yes I am.

"Did you know that every time you say her name, your body chemicals elevate?"

Robert sighed. *Med, please stop checking my vitals every time I either think about or am near Sarah.*

"Did you not want to know about–"

I know what I feel like at those times, Robert interrupted his companion.

"You wanna come for dinnah?"

I just don't need you whispering in my ear about it.

"I am not whispering in your ear. We have discussed this before. I am speaking to your mind telepathically."

Ackers sighed in frustration as he tossed the letter on the desk and began emptying some of his pockets. *In this case 'whispering in my ear' is a human idiom for someone or something that keeps nagging at you when you don't need the input or advice. Since I am not in a dangerous situation, I find it too invasive.*

"I see. Still it is helpful for me to understand how humans interact. How do you prepare for this 'date'? What are your customs for it?"

Jeepers, Med, you ask the darnedest questions! Right now I need to wash up, change my clothes, and make sure I get there on time.

"Is she not expected to do the same?"

In some cases yes. However, since I'm picking her up at her work, it will be okay since she obviously won't have had any opportunity to change. We're just going somewhere casual where we can sit and talk.

"So you do not necessarily expect her to abide by whatever conventions of dating she would normally be expected to honor?"

Not this time. We barely know each other. Please stop with the questions! I have a couple hours left and I'd like to get a little writing done. Ackers had put his glasses back on and was about to sit down at his desk when in the sudden silence he heard something outside.

What was that?

He ran to the closed window and peered out after picking up the sound of a scream somewhere nearby with his enhanced senses. Outside on the street he spotted a woman and a man struggling over a handbag.

The neighborhood he lived in was rather run down and prone to petty thefts as well as more serious crimes. Most people kept to themselves for fear of retaliation. Yet he now had the ability to defend and protect the innocent victims. Without a second thought to his own safety or requesting help from Med, Robert Ackers unlocked and unbolted his door and raced down the stairs.

Exiting the tenement, he saw the man and woman were still fighting over the bag, while several people stood around not knowing what to do. The man had a knife out and looked like he knew how to use it.

Ackers ran over and grabbed the man's knife hand, squeezing it far harder than a normal human would be capable of doing. Bones crunched and the man screamed in pain. He immediately released the bag to grab his limp and throbbing hand. Robert had him by the other arm immediately, wrenching it behind and twisting it up against the man's back. A couple other men stepped forward to help out, either emboldened or embarrassed now that the attacker was subdued by the mousy looking guy with the wire rimmed glasses. One man casually kicked the knife aside while the other stood before the would-be purse snatcher with his fists up, like he'd also been part of the fight.

"Are you alright ma'am?" Robert asked, not letting go of the stranger. It was his collar after all. "He didn't hurt you?"

"No, I'm fine, just a little shaky. He was trying to steal my bag and scare me in the process," she explained, glancing quickly over at the knife. "I was just paid by my employer and I think this jerk must have seen me cashing my check at the bank and followed me. He would have gotten a whole week's pay if you hadn't stepped in and saved me. Thank you."

"Glad I could help," Robert said warmly. "Here comes a police officer now," he added, noticing a foot patrol cop approaching. "Please file charges with him and get this creep arrested. You should have enough witnesses to make the charges stick," he added, looking around at the crowd and frowning. They hadn't done much before, so the least they could do now was back up her story.

"Hey, buddy, it was just a misunderstanding between me and her," the would-be thief complained. "And you broke my hand for nuttin'! I'm tellin' the copper that and you'll git arrested too. Be a long night in the holdin' cell with me if you don't let me go now. You might have a little accident—"

Ackers turned to face the man and smiled. "No. You're going to jail alone pal. These people saw what you did."

While they've been talking, the crowd had been thinning out as the cop came over. Nobody wanted to be involved. This guy might have connections with the local mobs.

"What's happening here?" the officer demanded.

"That dirty rotten thief," the woman began, pointing at the one Robert was holding, "he tried to steal my bag when this young man came over and stopped him."

The officer looked at Ackers. "He did, did he? Good for you pal. Glad somebody in this neighborhood has some moxie in 'em." He turned back to face the thief. "Oh we know this one. He's got a record as long as me leg. I'll take him into custody," he added, while pulling out his handcuffs as the wail of a siren sounded in the distance. "Ah, here comes your ride now." Having cuffed the man in spite of his protests over the broken hand, the officer turned his attention back to the woman. "Ma'am, if you'll come to the precinct with me and file a report, we'll get this crook into lockup for now and maybe the judge'll ship him out to a more permanent home up the river, as they say."

"I—" she glanced timidly at the now glowering purse snatcher and then at Robert Ackers, who smiled and nodded encouragement. "I can do that," she said with a lot more conviction in her tone than she had before.

"You'll be sorry lady!" the purse snatcher said, and the cop hauled off and clopped him upside the head with one fist.

"None of that now ya lousy mook," he warned.

Looking back at Robert, the officer asked, "What's your name and address Mister? For my report. You'll also need to come by as a witness, seein' as most of the other folks as was here before seem to have lost their nerve." It was true, just the three of them were standing on the side of the street.

Med began to say something but Robert mentally shushed him. "My name is Robert Ackers. I was on my way out to a meeting, but I can do that tomorrow since I need to come by the precinct to see Captain Rogen anyway. Someone left me a message about that today."

"Is that so? Okay Robert Ackers. Tomorrow then. I'm Officer Hadley," he pointed to his badge. "Please use that name when asking about the case," he requested as a squad car pulled up and another officer got out. "Let's go you," he said to his prisoner, propelling the man forward toward the curb.

"Hey, not so rough. I told you that creep Ackers broke my hand," protested the thief as the three of them walked away. "I'll get you for this Ackers!" he shouted, struggling between the two cops. "I know people who like to break heads on finks and do-gooders. Yer good as dead—OOF!" A billy club in the gut shut his mouth long enough to shove him in the back of the squad car.

As Robert Ackers proudly walked back to his apartment, ignoring the yelling behind him, Med observed, *Robert, I thought you needed anonymity when performing these acts? Why did you not ask me to 'light you up' this time?*

Ackers answered, *First because there was no time. Second, it really wasn't necessary. I was helping to stop a random crime with only one man armed with a knife, so the danger level was low. It was a situation where my identity didn't need to be hidden. In fact, I really didn't want to be Blue Light so close to where I live anyway. Someone might have seen me change shape and then they'd know it's really me.*

Med admitted to being confused. *"There are times when you need to mask your identity and others when you do not?"*

Yes Med, and I'll let you know which is which. Besides, you actually did help me.

"How? What did I do?"

Robert smiled. *You made me stronger and faster. I was able to render that thief helpless pretty easily, without struggling. Because of that I wasn't afraid to get involved like all those other people were, so I didn't need your other abilities this time.*

"I am glad I was able to help, even if it was unknowingly."

Well, it's taken some time for me to gain that kind of self-confidence. You know, I don't have time to do any writing now, although I think I'll scribble down some notes about this before I get ready for my date. Maybe I can incorporate it into a mystery or detective story.

"Another potential writing market to get into," Med said in an imitation of Robert's usual tone when talking about his career.

Exactly! You're learning Med. You're learning.

CHAPTER 8

Promptly at seven, showered and in fresh clothing, Robert walked into the diner and saw Sarah at the counter talking to the cashier. He waited nearby until they were done before he spoke up.

"Hello Sarah. Are you about ready to go?" he asked.

She turned and smiled. "Just a minute Robert. I need to get my coat."

"I'll be right here," he promised, as she walked away.

The cashier smiled at Robert and said, "Hello again Mr. Ackers. Are you taking Sarah out tonight?"

Robert answered, "Yes, Diana. Just out for coffee."

"Why go out for coffee?" Diana asked him. "We make a good cup right here."

"Yes you do, but I'd rather take her to someplace else for our first, uh, date."

Diana looked at him wistfully. "That's nice. My Oscar also took me out to a different place on our first date. Unfortunately, we don't go out as much now that I'm working full time."

While they were chatting, a man came in and after looking around to see who else was nearby, sauntered up toward the cashier's station. Growing impatient because he didn't know how much longer the lone man in the diner intended to keep yakking to the cashier, he took a gun out of his jacket pocket and pistol whipped Robert, knocking him to the ground.

Then he pointed the weapon at Diana and said, "Gimme all your dough, or you'll get worse than he did."

Diana shook nervously. "Y-y-yes sir," and pressed the button on the cashier box, which rang the bell as the drawer opened up. She started to collect all the cash as the thief leaned in and told her to hurry, while pointing the gun directly at her face.

"*Robert, can you hear me?*" asked Med. "*I am healing your injury as fast and efficiently as I can. What to you want me to do? Light you up?*"

Ackers groaned and thought, *No, not here. Can you create a small invisible tendril?*

"*Yes. Do you want me to utilize it to knock him to the floor?*"

No. Plug the barrel of the gun with it. Then cover the hand and gun completely, but keep it unseen so no one else notices. Then help me stand up.

Med sent out a clear appendage. It was not completely invisible, for upon careful scrutiny a faint outline of it was noticeable though the rest was completely clear. It covered both the gun and the hand holding it.

Then Med augmented Robert's own strength enough to help Ackers get off the floor.

"Hey buddy, watch where you point that thing," Ackers quipped to distract the would-be robber as he swayed on unsteady feet, fighting not to give in to unconsciousness. Med hadn't had enough time to completely heal him, and his head was swimming.

"Had to be a stinkin' hero," the gunman snarled as he whipped around, somewhat baffled to see his first victim upright again. "I'll plug yah this time so you'll stay down," he said confidently, pointing the weapon at Ackers and pulling the trigger as Diana screamed and dropped the cash she was holding in trembling hands, her face white as sheets and hands over her eyes.

Instead of firing, the pistol's barrel blew apart. All the debris and the bloody mess remained contained in Med's clear creation. The explosion was silenced inside the shielding so it hurt no one other than the gunman. The robber screeched in agony as he instinctively reached for his wounded hand with the other, but couldn't touch it because of the construction.

Med, release his hand.

"Yes Robert."

Ackers then swung his right fist and hit the man in the jaw, knocking him out.

Having heard the screams, Sarah came running out from the kitchen with her coat half on and waitress hat off, her hair falling down around her shoulders. She stopped a few feet away and just stared, open mouthed and speechless, from one man to another. Robert Ackers with his beaten bruised face and the strange man out cold on the floor, one hand blackened and bloody with the remains of a pistol nearby. Diana was in shock and shaking uncontrollably, where she peeped on over the counter and down at the now unconscious would be thief.

"You knocked him out," the cashier finally said in a high pitched tone on the edge of hysteria, yet filled with disbelief. "I thought for sure you were down for the count. I was afraid he would shoot us both but— What happened to his gun?"

"Guess he was in a hurry and didn't hit me hard enough," Robert said innocently, for Med was working to get him healing from the inside and he already felt far better. "I don't know about the gun, but I'd guess he didn't keep it in good shape. Damn thing blew up on him. Are you okay?"

"I am now," Diana said in a still quavering voice as Sarah came up to comfort her. "But he's bleeding all over the floor," she added with sick dread in her voice.

"I know. We need to call the police. Do you have a phone back there?"

"Only a pay phone over near the restrooms," Sarah told him as she made Diana sit down and whispered comforting words to her as the cashier put her head in her hands and began to sob.

"If you have Diana calmed down enough to leave her, could you call the police Sarah? I'll watch him in case he comes to."

"Sure, sure," she said and hurried around the counter toward the phone, but then stopped in her tracks to take a better look at both Robert and the unconscious man. "He's— in bad shape," she said a little uneasily, noting the blood pooling on the floor.

"Go make the call Sarah," he prompted her. *Med, once she leaves the room, can you keep him from bleeding out?* Robert was asking mentally when Sarah looked at him with the blood slowly dripping from his face where the blow from the pistol had caught him.

"I can only shut off the blood flow, I cannot heal his hand. And I will have to stop healing you to do that."

Fair enough! It was all the criminal deserved for what he had done. *You know, something just occurred to me Med. Do you think-*

"Oh, but you're hurt too—we'll also need an ambulance!" Sarah exclaimed and then rushed toward the back part of the restaurant.

"Just for him!" Ackers called after her, forgetting what he had been going to ask Med, who was now busy with an unseen tendril wrapped around the lower forearm of the still unconscious gunman.

After making the call, Sarah returned with a damp towel from the kitchen. After quickly checking on Diana, who had pulled herself together long enough to pick up the cash she had dropped and shut it back inside the register drawer, the young waitress started dabbing at Robert's face, which had stopped bleeding. The cuts were fairly well sealed and any bruising left was very light. "Maybe I was just rattled, but I swear you seemed to be more seriously hurt when I first saw you," she said with some surprise in her voice.

"I'm fine Sarah. He didn't hit me that hard and I'm a fast healer. I'll be alright," he said, covering for Med's influence. "That guy though—"

"He looks terrible but you're okay so I don't care," she said fiercely, still staring into Robert Ackers eyes and never once looking down at the unconscious man on the diner floor. "I still think you need to go to the hospital. It's only a few blocks. They can take him in the ambulance and I'll get us a cab."

"Don't bother Sarah," he protested. "I promise you, I'm okay. See? It's already stopped bleeding."

"I do see, but that brute hit you with... what? A gun across the face?"

Robert's silence confirmed her suspicions.

"You're bruised and cut. You really need to see a doctor."

"Sarah, I really don't think that's necessary-"

Sarah put her hands on her hips and said sternly, "Robert Ackers, if you're going to date me, you need to listen to what I say. I think you need to see a doctor and that's that. Understand?"

He raised his hands in surrender. "Okay, but not the hospital. I'll go to the doctor's office down the block tomorrow. Alright by you?"

"WE'RE going to the doctor together. Now," she said and stomped off to make another phone call.

"Robert, we do not need to see a medical professional," Med silently reminded him. *"Let me proceed and I will heal you more quickly and no scar will show when finished. You know I can do that."*

Ackers thought about it but then refused. *I know you can Med, but in this situation, it's important for Sarah to have her way. I don't want her to see the injury healing too quickly because then she will think something is wrong about me. And honestly, this isn't a bad way for us to get to know each other better.*

Med confessed to not understanding.

Sarah wants to help me. It's her way of showing me that she cares about me.

"You would prefer this even though I can do that faster and more completely?"

Ackers mentally sighed. *Yes. This is just something beyond your understanding right now. Sarah isn't aware of my—our—abilities and I want to keep it that way. Besides, I kind of like the idea. It might bring us closer.*

Diana spoke up, her voice sounding a bit stronger now. "Mr. Ackers, I can hear sirens, so the police are coming. I hope they take him away," she added, pointing toward the unconscious thief.

Sarah came back. "The police took my initial report over the phone when I called them, but they want you to stay here until they can ask you some questions. I told them you were injured and they said there will be medical personnel on the scene. I called the doctor's office anyway, and he will wait for us to call back." The firmness in her voice said she would not take no for an answer.

"Okay fine. When the ambulance comes they can look at it and bandage it up if they don't like it." *That should keep everyone satisfied,* he thought.

"*Robert. Before we were interrupted, you said you wanted to ask me something,*" Med reminded him.

Oh, right. I was wondering if you have any idea as to why my, or should I say our, encounters with crooks has dramatically increased since we met.

"All I can say is that when I was looking for someone compatible to work with, I sensed a great need for a positive influence in this area, although I am at a loss as to why. I see by your reaction that I was correct in my analysis that more violent acts are escalating."

Yeah they are. It's always been a dicey neighborhood, but never this bad. Something different is going on out there. But what?

"*I do not know the cause, but together we can be the solution,*" Med replied, to which Ackers silently agreed.

+++

A few minutes later an ambulance crew entered the diner. One man started looking over Robert as the other knelt down and examined the crook.

Then Officer Hadley walked in. He raised his eyebrows, obviously surprised to see Ackers. "You again? What happened this time?"

"I came in to pick up my date after work. That man came in. He was armed and tried to rob the cashier. He smacked me across the face with his gun then pointed it at Diana," he pointed to the uneasy cashier, "and demanded the money from the till. She had opened the register and was complying when I managed to get up off the floor. That's when he pointed the gun at me and pulled the trigger. Luckily for me it exploded in his hand. While he was recoiling from the shock I knocked him out."

"I see," the officer said, shaking his head in disbelief. "You certainly get around. Maybe I should call you Crime Stopper."

"Personally, I would prefer not to run into any of these messes at all and leave them for you," Robert replied, mentally shushing a protesting Med as he did. *We must remain anonymous!*

"Even if he wasn't out like a light, we'd still have to take him on a stretcher to the hospital because of that hand," the ambulance attendant looking over the would-be robber said as he stood up. "You really hit him hard," he said to Robert. "What did you use, a brick?"

"No. I got in a lucky punch because the guy was more worried about his hand," Ackers said.

"Can't blame him. He's probably going to lose it," the attendant said. "Bill, when you're done with him, can you go get the stretcher?"

"In a minute Charlie," his partner answered. "This guy needs some attention too. I don't think he needs stitches, but definitely a bandage."

With that, Officer Hadley informed Robert, "I'm afraid this time you do need to come to the precinct with me. I have to report this and I need you there." Before Ackers could protest, he waved him off. "Given the seriousness of these circumstances, tomorrow won't work."

"It can at least wait till he's bandaged up, can't it?" Sarah asked.

"Yes ma'am," Hadley told her politely.

"Well I'm coming with him," she added.

"You don't need to. We just need him to give a witness statement about this and the earlier incident also," Hadley explained.

Sarah's eyes turned toward Robert with a questioning look. "What earlier incident?" she said in an arch tone.

Robert looked down a little embarrassed. "Well, there was this woman who was having her purse snatched and I kinda got involved."

Sarah put her hands on her hips and in a stern voice asked, "Got involved how?"

Hadley grinned at Robert. He was going to get the third degree from more than one source tonight, but filled in the pertinent information for him. "Seems your boyfriend is on a bit of a hero streak today Miss. He stopped that purse snatcher and just about broke the man's hand in the process," he said before Robert could even speak.

Sarah looked at Robert in shock. "You did that and you didn't even tell me? Geez, I'll have to keep a close eye on you Robert Ackers. You know, you're gonna get hurt one of these days if you keep that up."

"*Do not worry Robert. As long as we are together, I will always protect you.*"

Robert mentally replied, *I know Med, but she doesn't know about you, and I want to keep it that way. At least for now.*

"*Maybe you should tell her. Then she might not be so fearful for your safety.*"

Not now, Med. Maybe later. Much later, Robert added, noticing how Sarah was staring at him with both awe and concern.

CHAPTER 9

"Sarge, I have a witness here to an attempted robbery at the diner downtown," Officer Hadley began, as he ushered Robert and Sarah into the precinct. "The same guy that also stopped that purse snatcher earlier today. When he's done giving his statements, he also needs to see the Captain. Is Rogen still in?"

Sarah turned to Robert, still holding his arm. "You need to see the Captain? Why?"

"An officer left a letter saying that their Captain wanted to talk to me, but it didn't say why. I was going to see him tomorrow so we could go out tonight."

Anger overtook Sarah's face. "Well maybe it was important Robert, since you seem to be some kind of local hero now. I sure hope this isn't going to happen all the time."

She looked distraught and Ackers didn't want to ruin what could be the beginning of a good relationship. "No Sarah, I swear it won't. And I honestly don't know why the Captain wants to speak to me." Thankfully she didn't know about the bank robbery because that had been handled by Blue Light.

Just then a man in uniform, with high ranking bars on his shoulders, came out of an office near the front desk.

"Was someone here to see me sergeant?" Captain Rogen asked.

The desk sergeant pointed at Robert. "Yes, sir. This man here. Says he got a letter saying you wanted to see him."

"Oh, What's your name?"

"Robert Ackers."

The captain smiled. "Ah yes. Please come into my office Mr. Ackers."

But before Robert could follow, Officer Hadley said, "Sir, he needs to give me a couple of witness reports too."

The captain's face turned a questioning glance at Hadley. "A couple?"

"Yes sir. A purse snatching a few hours ago in front of his tenement, and an attempted robbery about fifteen minutes ago at the diner where this young lady works."

"I see. So— he witnessed both of these situations?" Rogen said with a suspicious glance at Robert.

"Actually, he, um, well— he was involved in preventing both of them. That is, he stopped both guys from committing the crimes. Knocked the second one out cold," explained Hadley.

Rogen turned to fully face Ackers as he said, "Did he now? I'd really like to read those reports when they're completed. I'll send him out to you when I'm finished." Then the Captain spotted Sarah. "So you are with Mr. Ackers, Miss…?"

"My name is Sarah Baker. And yes, I'm with him," she replied proudly.

"Okay then Miss Baker. Please have a seat and if you have anything to add to what Mr. Ackers has told us, the officer behind the desk will give you a pen and a form to write on. I won't keep him but a few minutes," Rogen promised her.

Turning to Robert, he said, "Come with me, Mr. Ackers."

Captain Rogen led Robert through the secretary's work space and into his office and pointed him to a chair in front of the desk. Rogen walked around and opened a drawer as he sat down. "Do you know why I wanted to see you Mr. Ackers?"

Robert shrugged. "Not a clue sir."

"Well, there was a robbery at a bank earlier today. I think you were inside when it happened. Were you?"

Robert frowned. "Actually Captain, I was. I was standing at one of the counters to the side and started to make out a withdrawal slip when some men came in. I left as soon as I could get out of there."

"And in your hurry, you must have dropped this," Rogen said, pulling out the envelope with Ackers' story inside.

Robert's eyes lit up and he grinned. "Yes I did. You found it!"

"One of my officers did and gave it to me," the Captain explained, while handing it to his guest. "Now tell me all that happened."

Thankfully while he was getting ready to go out for the evening Robert had thought to come up with a plausible story if he was ever questioned about it.

"Well, as I said, I was in the bank when the men came in. As soon as I saw the guns, I ran out. Thankfully they didn't stop me so I kept running. By the time I found a pay phone I heard sirens so I figured the police were already on their way. Since I didn't see too much that would be helpful, I went on home," Robert added, embellishing his story. "It wasn't until I was halfway home that I realized I didn't have my manuscript anymore, but I figured it would be safer to go back to the bank tomorrow and ask if anyone found it."

"So you didn't see what happened next?" Rogen asked.

"No," Ackers said carefully. "Why? Was it something important?"

"The Blue Light," the Captain calmly answered.

Oh, that was why they wanted him to come in. Ackers kept his reaction under control, and acted puzzled. "What blue light? You mean like a store sign that lights up? I don't recall seeing any blue signs on or in the bank."

"Robert your respiration and hormone levels are rapidly rising!"

Shut up Med! He snapped mentally.

"No Mr. Ackers. I'm not talking about signs. Did you see a large blue glowing man in the bank?"

Robert sat back in his chair and started to laugh. "Is this some kind of joke?" When Rogen just glared at him, Robert said, "You can't be serious! If I saw something like that, I'd think I was losing my mind." Ackers sounded rattled even to his own ears.

Med, see if you can do something to calm my nerves, he pleaded. *Do it quietly, but fast!*

"I will do whatever I can manage," the medallion replied.

The Captain nodded affirmatively, his eyes narrowed in a raptor's gaze. "I never joke when I am interviewing witnesses Mr. Ackers. Please answer the question." He was watching Robert intensely.

Thankfully Med was able to calm his overreaction somewhat. "No sir, I didn't see a large blue man in the bank," Ackers said more calmly. "I'm quite sure I would have noticed someone like that if he had been there."

Rogen just said "Hmmm…" again, as he continued to study his guest.

"All right then. I find it interesting that you seem to have been in a lot of places where criminal activities were happening today. First the bank, then the purse snatching, then the attempted robbery at the diner. How is that happening Mr. Ackers?"

Med's influence was a great help. Robert felt almost relaxed as he shrugged and said, "I'm sure it's just a coincidence, Captain. It's not like I go out looking for trouble."

"Yes, but that's a heap of coincidences for one day."

"It looks to me like the crime rate is growing," Robert pointed out, before suggesting, "Maybe that's something you should look into. It seems like lately, you can't go two feet from your own residence without stumbling over something illegal. You aren't saying I shouldn't get involved, are you? That I should have let the man take the purse or the crook steal from the diner?"

"Not at all. Too many people just look on or walk away as it is. However, getting involved could get you hurt," the Captain reminded him, while pointing at Robert's bandaged face.

'Robert, does he suspect we are Blue Light?' Med asked in a concerned tone of voice.

No, Ackers silently replied. *I do think he believes I know more than I'm saying, but he doesn't suspect that. Not yet, anyway.*

"I'm just wondering," Rogen began, unknowingly interrupting the silent conversation, "where were you a couple of nights ago? Were you near an alley on Fifth? Or an accident on Main?"

Robert knew what the Captain was suspicious of, and looked thoughtful before replying, "A couple of nights ago? Well, I'm usually at home writing. A couple of nights ago I was probably working on the story in this envelope." He patted it. "I'm a writer," he added with a grin. "I've had a few pieces published in science fiction magazines. This one is something new I'm trying for a different market. A mystery."

"I see." Rogen figured he was one of those people who wanted to see what the crime world was like from the inside. He'd be lucky if he didn't get himself killed in the process. "Well, thank you Mr. Ackers. I think that will be all for today. Do be careful out there. You seem to find a lot of trouble, and much of it could be dangerous to you. Let the police handle it from now on." Rogen added, standing to indicate the meeting was over.

"Sure, Captain," Robert said as he started to rise. "I'll try to stay clear of any further issues. And thanks for returning my story."

As he turned to walk to the office door, Robert heard the Captain say,

"Mr. Ackers, if you ever need to speak with someone about anything—ANYTHING at all—come see me."

Robert turned back briefly to face the other man. "If I need any help I definitely will. Bye sir, and thanks again."

He went out the door and spotted Sarah still sitting on the bench. She smiled sweetly at him, but with obvious concern. "Is everything okay Robert?"

"Yes. The captain wanted to give me this," showing her the envelope, "and ask a few questions about events today."

"What is that?"

"It's a story I wrote and was getting ready to mail when I dropped it. The police found it."

"A story?"

"Yes. I'm a writer. I'm glad I got it back. I'll mail it out to a potential publisher tomorrow."

She smiled again. "That's nice. I didn't know you were a writer. Have you been doing it long?"

"A bit. Been successful with it, too. I've several stories published and gotten paid pretty well for them. Um, where is Officer Hadley? He wanted me to fill out those witness reports. After I'm done here, if you still want, we can go out for that coffee. And maybe something to eat now. I don't know about you, but I'm hungry."

Sarah smiled back at him, "Oh, yes me too, please."

+++

A very self-satisfied Robert was back in his apartment after a pleasant meal and some good conversation. Despite the day's events, he and Sarah had really hit it off, and they agreed to go out again some time. It was a positive ending to a trying day.

Now Med had some questions, and Robert was relaxed enough to answer them, grateful that he could do so silently in the dark with his eyes closed.

"That was a most interesting conversation, yet all the two of you did was talk. Is that the only component to this dating?"

It's a start Med. After our next date we will probably feel more comfortable with each other.

"What will happen then?"

We'll probably talk more. If I'm lucky, I might get a kiss.

"And this is how you procreate?"

Now in his pajamas in bed, Robert rolled on his side and sighed. *This was just the beginning of our dating Med. First we have to get to know each other. We do that by talking about our experiences, hopes and dreams, plans for the future. Then, if we both agree, it can go on to more— physical activities. Eventually, if it goes well, we fall in love, get married, and it moves on from there.*

"Exactly what moves on from there?"

That was getting intrusive. Robert wasn't ready to think that far ahead. *We can talk about that later Med. For now I think we need to figure out how to handle Captain Rogen.*

"What do you mean by handle?" Med seemed confused.

It's obvious that he's at least curious about my sudden crime fighting and the Light's arrival at the same time. Even if he doesn't suspect an actual connection between the two events yet, I'd rather he not get any closer to the truth. If he or anyone else discovers I'm Blue Light, it's going to make it impossible for me to have a real life outside of fighting crime.

"Understood, but how do we prevent that?"

Well that was no help!

That will take some thought. For now, I've had a long day and I need sleep, if I can get any. I'm still pumped up from the time with Sarah.

"Is that a normal reaction for a first date?"

I suspect so, though I don't have a lot of experience there. When you have intense feelings for someone, as I do for Sarah, it's exciting. You couldn't tell by my body's reactions?

"You told me no monitoring when not in danger."

Wow! You actually listened to something I said. Thank you for that. Now good night Med.

"Rest well Robert."

CHAPTER 10

While the just and weary took their well-deserved rest, there were others in the world who did their dirty deeds under the cover of darkness.

That very night, in the back office of a building near a train underpass, a short man with a cigar dangling from his mouth looked up from whatever was on his desk when there was a furtive rap on his door.

"Come in!" he barked at whoever was waiting outside.

A roughly dressed man opened the door and peered inside. "Hey Boss, Mickey's here."

"Mickey? Oh yeah, the bank job. About time he showed up. Bring him in, Stan."

Stan ushered the only man who managed to get away from the bank robbery fiasco into the office and, remaining inside in case he was needed, closed the door behind them.

The Boss shot a flat-eyed appraisal at his underling, saying nothing, letting him squirm a bit. Then with a slight smile that held no warmth, he asked, "So, Mickey. Where've you been? That bank job went down hours ago. How much did you get?"

Mickey knew the Boss was well informed and he was just playing the game. They all thought he'd just run off after the job went sour. Mickey had seriously thought about doing just that, but he'd been around long enough to know what happened to deserters once they were hunted down, so he'd come in to report instead, hoping for some leniency. "Look Boss, I had ta take da long way 'round 'cause I di'n't wanna be follad. At least they di'n't get me."

The Boss, hearing the edge in Mickey's answer, glared at him. "You didn't want *who* to get you?"

Mickey started visibly shaking as he mumbled, "Da coppers fer sure, but specially dat blue guy."

Now the Boss was getting aggravated. He couldn't stand cowards. "I didn't hear you so clear there Mickey. What did you say?"

Scared, Mickey yelped, "That glowin' blue guy, Boss. He was wipin' the floor wit' dem udder mugs. I barely got away."

The Boss angrily rose from his chair and pointed his cigar at Mickey. "So— you're telling me a glowing blue guy got involved with the bank job?"

Mickey nervously looked behind him, hoping for some support. Stan just stared back, not showing any expression. With that, the man turned and said, "Look, I swear it's da truth. 'E came outta nowhere all lit up bright blue. The boys shot at 'im but he stopped all the bullets somehow. Den 'e slammed me down—hard. The others couldn't get away but I seen some tools by where dey was fixin' the front of the bank so I grabs a sledge and I hit 'im hard enough to make my hands hurt. It connected solid, and I thought I got 'im, but he slammed me away again and I'm lucky I didn't break my neck. I run just as the cops was getting there. I thought I was gonna get caught, but I ran into an alley and hid wherever I could ta make

"So Mickey, where've you been?"

sure I wasn't follad."

The Boss' faced turned red as he failed to keep the rage out of his voice as he stalked back and forth like a caged lion. "So you're telling me this Blue Light thing stopped the robbery and all the others were caught? That we didn't get any money?"

Mickey was barely able to breathe as he said, "Yeah Boss, that's 'ow it all went down. Not a cent."

The Boss had been prepared to off Mickey for being a deserter, but now he was a needed witness. So he started a private rampage to work off steam. He threw his chair toward the far wall before sweeping all the papers and other items off the desktop. The phone rattled and dinged as it hit the floor. It helped calm him down so he could think rationally. He puffed his cigar back to life and exhaled a cloud of smoke.

"Damn it all! We had a good thing going here! Now all of a sudden it's Blue Light this and Blue Light that." He turned to face his two subordinates. "We gotta nab this Blue Light creep pronto and make him very dead. Stan, you take Mickey here and a few others. Find out who this Blue Light character is and where he hangs out without spooking him, and then report back to me. I got someone in mind who will make sure the job's done and done right! Understand?"

Stan, taken aback by the ferocity of the boss' anger, hastily replied, "Sure Boss. Right away."

"And send Sammy in on your way out."

"You got it Boss," Stan said in a carefully controlled tone before grabbing a shaking and speechless Mickey by a shoulder. Propelling him around he opened the door and they both left quickly before the Boss changed his mind.

A minute later another man walked in. He was tall and well dressed, smoking a cigarette in an ivory holder. A real cool character. "You wanted to see me, Boss?"

Calming down, the Boss retrieved his chair and said, "Yeah Sammy, sit down."

Sitting again, the Boss placed his elbows on the desk and said, "Give me the full report of the day."

Sammy removed his cigarette, using the time to compose his thoughts before saying, "Well, three of the snatches went off without a hitch. Two didn't because cops were around, so nothing went down."

"That was smart of those guys to back off, but that's only five. Didn't you send out six crews?"

Sammy, having been warned by Stan that the Boss was aggravated, steeled himself before answering. "Ah, yes, the sixth. That was Butch. He got pinched and is in the hospital handcuffed to a bed. The police are waiting to arrest him."

"Butch got pinched?" The Boss asked in disbelief. "Why? He didn't see the cop and tried to do the snatch anyway?"

Sammy looked down at his smoking cigarette. This was going to get hard to explain and not sound batty. "It wasn't a cop that caught him."

"Not a cop?" The Boss' face was getting flushed again "What happened Sammy?"

"As I understand it, Butch yanked on an old lady's purse and made to run with it, but she wouldn't let go and started screaming. They were playing tug of war and he'd almost got it when this guy comes out of nowhere and grabs his arm. Butch took a swing at the guy, but the do-gooder caught the fist and started squeezing. Butch went down with a broken hand, the guy crushed it. At that point a cop had come up and took over. So Butch went to the hospital under guard and the guy walked away, promising he'd be by the precinct tomorrow to file a witness report."

"You're saying some beefy good Samaritan type just suddenly showed up and stopped the snatch?"

Sammy stared at the Boss and said as calmly as he could, "Yes. Just showed up and helped the old broad. But he wasn't big or strong. Some average Joe with glasses."

The Boss sat back in his chair with a dumbfounded look on his face. "Well, I guess it had to happen sometime." *At least it wasn't that damn Blue Light this time.* "Okay, we got three of these rich old dames' purses when they were stuffed with cash. So our inside information is legit. Still, we got to have more than just this chicken feed to send uptown if we want to stay in the game. So what's up next?"

"Well, on the West Side we sent out a few guys to pick up money from the stores paying protection. Did the job and came back. No problems. The owners seemed properly manageable and just forked it over."

"As well they should be," replied the Boss, happy that something went right. "Good. That leaves the… Oh yeah. The diner job. The one where the owner wouldn't pay protection and we sent someone to boost him so he'd think twice next time it was offered. Who'd we send?"

"Alfie."

"Alfie, good. How much did he get?"

"Well—"

The Boss, getting agitated again, pointed at Sammy and scowled. "Look, I'm tired of this nonsense. Spit it out. What happened?"

"Alfie got pinched too."

The Boss appeared mad enough that steam might come out of his ears like in one of those comedic shorts. He closed his eyes and with cold deliberation slowly asked, "What happened?"

"Alfie goes in about closing time. He smacks down a customer across the face with his gun, then points it at the cashier. She opens the cash box when suddenly the guy gets up from the floor. Alfie points his gun at him and pulls the trigger."

Following the conversation, the Boss nodded and said, "So the guy gets shot. Alfie runs out of the diner and gets pinched by a cop passing by who heard it. Right?"

Sammy shook his head. "Not exactly. The gun exploded in Alfie's hand. Strange thing. It seemed like the explosion was contained somehow. Anyway, Alfie grabs for his injured hand and the guy punches Alfie, who goes down like a ton of bricks, out cold. They call the cops."

"Are you saying one more stinking good Samaritan stopped another job? Two guys on the same day?"

Sammy hesitated before saying, "Something like that."

The Boss pounded his fists on the desk. "What do you mean? Look, this is costing us time and money we can't afford to lose. Just give me the straight story."

Sammy had purposely saved the best for last in case the Boss was irritated enough to want to make an example of someone. He didn't want it to be him. "The diner job was stopped by the same guy who stopped Butch from getting the old lady's purse."

The Boss went quiet, staring at Sammy in stunned silence.

"You're telling me the same guy stopped both jobs?" was the question when he found his voice again.

"Yes," Sammy replied, staring right back at him.

The Boss sat silently at his desk for a few minutes.

Then he looked calmly back at Sammy and asked, "Did the gun jam or something?"

"The police think either that or it was a defective bullet. Either way, the other man was really lucky."

"Not for long," the Boss said. "Do we know who this guy is?"

"Yes, I did some digging, made a couple calls and just found out. After the ambulance people bandaged him up he went to the precinct. When he and this girl came out he was carrying an envelope I heard they were holding for him. One of my smarter picks had seen the name on the return address. His name is Robert Ackers. We know where he lives now too. The Mondella building."

The Boss smiled; he recognized the name 'Mondella'.

"Oh, that's real fortunate Sammy. We need to send a message to Mr. Ackers *and* his landlady. One that the rest of the people in his building won't ever forget. I want this done publicly—very messy, and *very* dead. You hear me? I not only want them dead, I want there to be no doubt as to why they're singing with the angel choir, as long as there's nothing that the cops can use to point back to whoever actually does the job. Anybody else interferes—off them."

Sammy gave the Boss a cold smile. "I thought you might want it that way. The only question is, when?"

"As soon as possible."

CHAPTER 11

Deep within a moonless night, Ackers was sound asleep when Med demanded, *"Robert! Wake up, WAKE UP!"*

Groggy, Robert turned toward the nightstand Med was resting on. *What is it?*

"There are some men outside your door. I've scanned them. They have guns."

Robert fully regained consciousness at that statement. *What? How do you know?*

"The same way we navigated while I deflected light around you at the bank, using energy transmissions for echolocation. They can penetrate the walls and doors."

You do this every night? Ackers asked, as he quietly scrambled out of bed.

"I don't need to sleep, so I keep watch all the time. For example, I know that besides the two men with guns in the hall outside, there is one on the street under your window."

Is that so? Do you think the ones in the hall will try to enter? He was trying to find his clothing without turning on a light.

"Yes. What will you do?"

I have to get dressed. Then I think we'll go out the window.

"But there is–"

Another one out there, I know. But if you surround me with that deflection shield without the light, we can jump down on him and he won't see me, right?

"I can arrange that as I guide us down."

Can you regulate how fast I can fall?

"Yes. How hard do you want to land on him? I have a full charge now and can perform limited levitation to insure your safety."

You can do that? Why didn't you tell me? Robert had fumbled into his clothing and was trying to get socks and shoes on.

"You had not asked me to do that before."

Med, we definitely need to talk some more about all the things you can do, but for now do the light deflection thing. The window's already open for the night breeze so I can just step out and fall. Slow me down just enough to knock the guy out and not kill him or myself from the fall. Fully dressed, he crept to the window and levered himself up on the sill.

"Ready when you are."

Do it now.

And with that, Robert Ackers simply disappeared.

+++

He dropped out of the third floor window and aimed for the man in the fedora beneath it. The man was looking up, but never saw anything amiss.

Med slowed down Ackers' descent as promised.

Still the man was struck hard on the head and shoulders and slumped to the ground unconscious.

Ackers grabbed the man's gun out of his hand and threw it into the storm drain.

Okay Med, now light me up full blue.

"Done," the medallion answered, as the darkness was diminished by the light. "What will you do now?"

I'm going after the two men in the hall, but we're going to let this one escape.

"Why?"

We'll go invisible again and follow him back to his hideaway so we can try to survey the place and see who else is a part of this. These mugs can't be the whole gang and they're a little too interested in me. I want to catch the rest of them, but for now we'll just rush up the stairs and surprise those hoods trying to get the drop on me.

"*But the front door is locked. If we crash through it, will not the noise alert them you are coming?*"

It's locked? Why would they— Oh God, they must have picked the lock, and locked it back up again because they planned on taking more than just me out! Can you form a key?

"*Yes. As you would say: let's do this!*" Med lit him up in the empty, predawn street.

That's the spirit!

+++

Blue Light moved to the front door and waited while a portion of his ethereal body flowed out into the lock.

As a click sounded, the appendage reformed to turn the knob and pushed the door open.

A bright blue shrouded form sped up the steps and saw only an empty hall, for his door was now unlocked and ajar. Maybe they had come and gone?

He was about to enter the apartment when he heard a low voice say, "Ackers ain't in here."

So they were still inside. Good!

The Blue Light took a position blocking the only sensible way out as the first man complained, "Look, we was told he was home t'night. Did yah check careful? He might be hidin' somewhere."

"This rat hole ain't that big," the other man insisted as they started to walk back into the hallway. "He's gone. Musta slipped past us."

"No friggin' way," his companion insisted as they moved to open the door, only to see a huge blue man blocking their exit.

Instinctively the hoods drew out their guns and managed to get off one shot each before two huge blue arms grabbed them and yanked them both through the door and up against the hallway wall with a loud crash.

Apartment doors opened up and down the hallway as curious people looked out. Some were ready to complain about the noise when they saw the two gunmen on the floor and a man shaped blue light standing over them.

A mechanical sounding voice emerged from within the light, telling everyone, "Go back into your rooms. Everything is under control.

Someone please call the police to come take these men away."

With that a huge blue glowing hand held the two men down. Another collected their guns while a third appendage extruded and pointed at one man before he went back inside his apartment.

"Excuse me, sir?" the artificial voice said. "Do you have anything I can bind these men with?"

The guy looked around and saw he was the only one still outside his room. "M-me?"

"Yes, you. Do you have anything I can bind these men with?" Blue Light asked.

"Well, I don't have any rope. I do have some metal bands I got from work that I was gonna give my brother. But they're thick and I don't know what you can do with 'em."

"They will be fine. Please get them for me."

The man went into his apartment and returned with two metal bars. Each was roughly fourteen inches long, two inches wide, and an inch thick.

"Here we are, but how will you—"

The man watched in astonishment as Blue Light easily bent a bar around each gun man's wrists into makeshift shackles to fasten them behind their backs. "Oh—wow—" the man said, backing away, both awed and a little frightened.

"That should hold them." Blue Light turned back to the now quaking man who was edging away from him. "Now, if no one else has already done so, please phone the police. I need to go."

"Uh, sure. I'll do that," came the answer in a small shaky voice.

"Thank you citizen." With that Blue Light turned and flowed back down the stairs, but as he was going out the front door, Ackers said, *Med, turn off the light.*

"*Will you not be in danger if I do so?*"

The man shaped form stood in the open doorway and thought, *Perhaps, but I can't follow him if I'm all lit up. He'll see me and so will anyone else passing by.*

"*Have you forgotten I can deflect light around you? He will not see you.*"

Oh, yeah, right. It had been a rude awakening and the adrenaline rush had made thinking harder. Plus this was still all new. *But I won't be able to get too close or I'll spook him. Can you follow him and not lose him in a crowd?*

"*You should have developed some trust in my abilities by now Robert. Believe me, I will not lose him.*"

Okay. He's finally getting up. Do it.

And with that, Blue Light disappeared once more, and so did Robert Ackers.

┿┿┿

The gunman on the ground slowly rose, having no idea what happened. *What the hell hit me?* He wondered, looking around. There was nothing to see. No one anywhere on the street, no fallen bricks or potted plants, and no sign of his companions.

Yet his gun was missing. He felt all over himself and hunted the area around him. Nothing! He figured somebody in this low-rent neighborhood must have come up silently behind and cold-cocked him to get his gun. His first thought was to check in with the other two mugs, but the wail of a siren in the distance made him change plans quickly.

Slowly—stumbling as if drunk—the man reluctantly limped away down the empty street. With each step he felt stronger and more like himself as his head cleared, never realizing he was being followed.

In his profession the hired gunman was cautious and checked behind him occasionally, but there was no one there. Still, he traveled through a number of streets, turning at multiple corners and even backtracked over his route a couple of times for good measure. You couldn't be too careful, especially without your side piece.

Yet despite his precautions, a now invisible Blue Light had continued to follow.

"*Robert, I still have some concerns about this situation,*" Med mentally announced.

Such as?

"*How will you explain your absence at your residence?*"

Not sure. Obviously I wasn't home. Maybe I can say I decided to stay somewhere else tonight.

"*With Sarah?*"

NO! Robert shouted in his head, then apologized for the outburst. *That wouldn't be appropriate. Sarah's not that kind of girl and I don't want to use her as an excuse. We've only had the one date and I can't ruin her reputation or endanger her under any circumstances. If anyone asks, I'll just say I couldn't sleep and went out for a walk. That way if someone actually saw me come home, they'd understand why I wasn't there when those goons broke in.*

"Understood." Med shifted Ackers' position to follow the man they were tracking. *"What will you do once this man has reached his destination?"* Med queried

I'll let you know when I know, was the honest answer.

+++

After another mile of walking, the gunman approached a building via a set of steps that went below the sidewalk level. He knocked on the door at the base of the stairs using a specific pattern.

Before the last knock had faded, a peephole opened and a pair of narrow eyes stared at him as a man's voice said, "Yeah?"

"It's me, Grover. I need to speak to Sammy."

After a few seconds, the door opened. Grover was ushered inside. The man paused to check the street to make sure no one might have seen him, but before the door closed again, the invisible Blue Light was now inside too.

Grover walked into the basement level office and spotted Sammy. The other man was sitting in an armchair underneath a single bulb. He'd been reading the newspaper, one knee crossed over the other, his ivory cigarette holder resting on top of an ashtray sitting on the nearby lamp table, smoke spiraling out of the lit cigarette. Sammy's weapon sat next to it.

"Sammy," the new arrival called out quietly so that he'd get his attention. You didn't want to surprise anybody down here.

Sammy looked up and gave a brief smile. "Grover. You're back quicker than I thought. Did you mess him up good before you killed him?"

"Um, well, I was the outside man, but I dunno because the guys you sent in didn't come back out."

"What?" Sammy said in shock, nearly shouting as he dropped the paper while his hands gripped the chair arms and his thin legs unfolded like a jackknife. "What happened to them?"

Grover, trembling, nervously replied, "I don't know. I heard a ruckus as I was getting up, but didn't see anyone."

Sammy eyed him, curious as he straightened up in the chair and asked, "As you were— getting up— What do you mean 'getting up'?"

Grover was becoming antsy, beginning to squirm. "Well, I was outside like I said when, it was like something crashed down on me. Whatever it was it— it knocked me out for a bit."

"Just exactly what knocked you out?" This made no sense and Sammy was getting irritated.

Grover trembled even more but managed to answer. "I don't know! I didn't see anything. One second I was outside below the mook's window and the next I was out. It felt like someone dropped a piano on me, yet there was no sign of anything when I got up."

Sammy picked up his cigarette holder and took a puff to calm his nerves. "I see. So how long were you out?"

Grover looked around nervously. "Couldn't have been more'n a few minutes."

"So what happened when you came to?"

"Well," began Grover, thinking quickly, "I heard noises coming from the apartment you sent us to. They staged me outside because Ackers had left his window open, but he never came out it." Grover paused before adding, "It sounded like a fight up there. I also heard a couple of gun shots too."

"Did you wait after the shots for the boys or anyone else to come out?" Sammy wanted to know.

"Yeah I did wait some, but no one come out. I couldn't stay too long though. Somebody must've called the cops. I heard sirens coming so I beat feet out of there."

"Well, at least you did that correctly," Sammy conceded. "You weren't followed, were you?"

"Naw, I looked all around. Zigzagged and everything. Even turned down a bunch a streets I didn't have to take before I came here."

"All right," Sammy said, thinking over what Grover had said.

The gunman got nervous but tried not to fidget while the other man just sat there eyeballing him. Then Sammy finally rose and said, "Wait here." He went over and knocked on the office door in the back of the room.

When a voice within finally said, "Come in," Sammy entered, closing the door behind him.

Within his office, the Boss was sitting behind his desk reading some papers. Smoke from a cigar in his right hand lazily drifted towards the ceiling. He looked up at Sammy and, noting the worried frown, set his papers down and took a drag on the cigar after knocking the excess ash off. Exhaling another cloud of smoke, he sat back and said, "So spill it already."

"It's the Ackers job," Sammy announced. "Something went sideways."

"What do mean, 'went sideways'?" the Boss asked in a menacing tone, while shoving his papers into a pile on the desktop.

"Grover just came back alone. Claims he was the lookout for this one and got knocked out, but he's pretty sure Ackers never got past him. When he came to he heard a ruckus and some gunshots, but the other guys didn't come back out. Unfortunately the cops showed up so he couldn't stay to see what was going down. He came back here by a roundabout route and claimed he wasn't followed."

"Okay, so do we know if–"

The Boss would never finish his question, for a bright flash of blue light appeared under the door, heralding a crashing sound in the outer room. This was followed by gunshots and different voices yelling things like, "Get him! Shoot him! Aargh!"

Sammy drew his pistol but then all went deathly quiet as the light disappeared.

"Maybe he left," Sammy said.

"Maybe," the Boss said grimly as he lifted something into his lap. He didn't get to be boss by taking chances.

The door came crashing inward. Splinters and chunks of broken wood flew everywhere as the huge form of Blue Light barged into the room and stood menacingly before the two remaining gangsters.

"It's you!" the Boss snapped with a toothy grin around the cigar clamped in his jaw. "I hear you've been interfering in my business. Well, you're gonna die now." He lifted a Tommy Gun with a twenty round box magazine full of ammunition. Without a second thought to his own safety, he set it to continuous discharge and started firing at Blue Light.

Sammy hit the floor to be out of the way of ricochets as the gun spit bullets and hot, spent brass. The acrid smell of gunpowder and the deafening sound of constant gunfire filled the room till the magazine was emptied.

The barrage was enough to stagger Blue Light, who initially careened backwards, its outer light dimming a bit. Thinking himself victorious, the Boss set the now empty weapon on the desk top and glared defiantly at what he thought was the wreckage of the current hero.

Then his face lost all color, shocked to see the blue form still standing! In fact, every single bullet was floating within the outer blue nimbus of the over size figure, which was growing brighter again as it gradually began moving forward. The bullets seemed to ooze out of that light and they dropped to the floor with a clatter.

"H-How the hell did that happen?" the Boss demanded to know. "I riddled you with enough lead to take down an elephant!"

A mechanical voice replied, "Guess I'm harder to kill than an elephant."

The Boss rushed around the desk, pulling a switchblade knife out of his pants as he ran. "Yeah we'll see about that," as he plunged it down into the huge blue form in front of him.

Blue Light never moved as the blade slipped through the outer glow, the tip nearly reaching the man within.

+++

That almost got me! Robert Ackers yelped to Med.

"*I am sorry Robert, but while I did absorb all the bullets, my energy level dropped doing so. That blade was very sharp and between the two factors I could not totally stop it.*"

Well, get him away from me at least, Ackers insisted.

Blue Light swept an arm outward, throwing the Boss very hard against a wall.

Sammy, who'd been commando crawling toward the open doorway since the Tommy gun stopped firing, got up and ran for his life.

"*Robert, that other man is escaping. Do you want to stop him?*"

No. He's going somewhere and I want to follow him. Is the other guy down?

"*Yes. He is knocked out,*" Med reported.

I see some filing cabinets in that corner. Can you look through the drawers and see what's on the papers inside?

A blue ray spread out from where Ackers was standing to shine on the file cabinets. "*There are multiple lists of people. The file folder on one says PROTECTION. Another says JOBS and one of the papers inside has the diner's name on it and–*"

And what Med? Ackers asked.

His partner hesitated before saying, "*There is also a list of HITS, with every name crossed out but yours.*"

Med sensed Robert's anger rise at that announcement. *So tonight at my place was planned?* Robert realized.

"*It appears so, but we stopped them,*" Med gently reminded him.

True, but I've drawn enough police attention as it is. Can you safely erase my name without damaging the rest of the list?

"*The writing of your name appears to be a more recent addition. I might be able to absorb the ink.*"

DO IT!

With that, Med was silent for a moment before announcing the task accomplished.

Then Blue Light pointed to the desk and said, *There's a phone. Can you dial the operator and inform them to bring the police here? I don't want to unmask if I don't have to.*

"Yes. I can create a modulation mimicking a human voice."

While you're doing that, I'm going to use that metal chair to bind this guy. When we're finished, we do the invisibility thing and follow the one who just left.

"How will that be possible? He has a head start that is steadily increasing."

I have an idea. I'll tell you when we get outside.

+++

An invisible Blue Light stepped onto the sidewalk as a police siren in the distance grew closer.

Okay Med. Can you extend yourself to the roof and pull me up?

"Of course." Med quickly created a strong tendril that attached to the roof with a sucker-like device and pulled Robert up safely. "I take it you want to look for him from above."

Yes, if you can recognize him. I can't see anything in this form, remember?

"Of course I can see, but if I leave to search for him, you will be unprotected."

I know! Could you extend a portion of yourself above me and look around, like a periscope. Ackers pictured a periscope device and Med was quick to catch on.

"I understand what you are suggesting, but I have a counter suggestion. Noting how a periscope works, I can improve upon it by creating a mirror system that will allow you to see through my extension. Wherever you turn, so will the focus of my extension, so that you can see outward also. In hindsight, we could have done that in the bank," Med added as it was forming the periscope system.

Actually, we couldn't chance it there, Robert replied. *If you'd created a mirror system, wouldn't anyone else also see the mirror looking out, making that portion of you visible? And someone looking in that direction might be able to look inside and see me.*

"I see the flaw in my design but we can use it now, being above street level with no one looking our way."

Fine. How far up can you extend it?

"A long distance. The energy tendril needed does not have to be thick."

Good, said Robert, looking through the viewing system. *Ah yes, in that direction. A man walking fast and constantly looking behind him. He's dressed like the one who left the office and there are not too many people out and about yet. Can we follow him over the roofs?*

"Yes. I will just extend my legs to cross the buildings, alleyways, and streets. You can keep him in sight."

CHAPTER 12

An invisible Blue Light followed Sammy until he entered an all night diner that served anyone from dock workers to cops on the beat. Ackers thought it was an odd place for the gangster to go.

Standing on top of that building's roof, Robert mentally asked, *Can you extend a tendril inside to see what he's doing? I need to know why he's here.*

"I can, but the mirror system will not work without a straight line of sight. There would be too many curves for that process."

I see. Hmmm… Then what about audio? You know, create a microphone for us to listen with. Keep it invisible.

"Your mind is everything I had sensed it would be. Wonderfully imaginative. Yes, I can do that." Med extended a threadlike thin line out of his light construct body down into the diner via a duct.

Can you screen out the background noise and just pick up what our guy is saying and who he might be talking to?

"I am working on that," Med answered. The audio came in low but clear.

"Hey Sammy, you're out late. What can I do for you?" a male voice asked.

"I need to make a call," the man they had followed from the gang's place said. His voice was easily recognizable. "When I get off the horn, can I get a tuna salad on rye?"

"Sorry, no more rye until my delivery in the morning. How about white?"

Sammy sighed and replied, "Yes, that's fine. I'll only be a minute."

The sounds of Sammy entering and closing a phone booth could be heard. Yet the audio continued as Med snaked the thin tendril under the door to let them hear the call.

"Hey Booker? It's me. I need to talk to Beta. Yeah, it's important. Okay, I'll hold."

A minute later the rooftop listeners heard, "This is Sammy. Ricco just got pinched. No, not by the cops, by Blue Light, but I bet the cops will show up again. Yeah, the one Ricco told you about. He crashed in from nowhere and took out anyone else who was there. I got out while the Light was taking down Ricco. I took a few turns to lose anyone who might follow. Yeah, I'm at Eddy's, just around the corner. I can sit tight here. You're sending a car? Twenty minutes? Sure that's fine, I'm getting a sandwich."

"I apologize for us only being able to hear his side of the conversation Robert."

That's okay. We heard far more than I hoped to. Ackers was already mulling over what had been said. This Beta had to be an alias for someone very important, well over the gangland boss Ricco.

"What is our next course of action?"

We wait for someone to come for Sammy. Then we follow them to this Beta's place. I think he might be the one who is behind this recent escalation of crimes in the area. Sounds like this Sammy reports to him, so we got lucky that he's the one who escaped. I'd like to know how far I can go up the chain of command with these crime lords, Ackers added, as they heard Sammy exit the phone booth and sit at the counter.

"Everything okay Sammy?" the other man asked.

"Huh? Oh, yeah," Sammy answered, sounding distracted. "How's the sandwich going?"

"Coming right up. Anything to drink with that?"

"Yes, a pop with ice."

"You got it. Here yah go. Soda in a second."

That's enough audio for now, Robert Ackers told Med.

With that, Med retrieved his audio tendril unnoticed.

+++

They watched from the roof top. After twenty minutes Robert started getting a little nervous, despite the fact that Sammy had yet to leave.

In another five minutes a dark car pulled up in front of the diner.

Get me some more audio, Ackers told Med.

A perfectly dressed man—wearing a gray pinstriped suit, white shirt, solid gray tie with matching fedora and black patent leather shoes with spats—got out from the driver's side and walked in. He spotted Sammy at the lunch counter and approached just as the other man was finishing his meal.

"Hey, Sammy."

Sammy turned around, startled to see who was there. He got up after leaving money on the counter for his meal, and said quietly as he approached the man, "Booker, he sent you? I expected someone like Ike."

"Yeah, he sent me. Any problems with that?" Booker asked as they headed for the door.

"No, not at all. Let's go," Sammy said.

"This is the end of the audio Robert, unless you want me to closely pursue them."

No, save your energy Med. Let's follow from up here, see where they go.

The two men went outside and once in the car, drove away.

+++

They were less than a block before Sammy looked around the area and asked, "Ah, Booker, aren't we headed in the wrong direction?"

"Nah. We're just gonna take the long way around to lose any tail you might have brought along," the other man replied.

"Look, I made sure nobody followed me," Sammy insisted.

"Yeah, well I was told to make double sure. You said Grover wasn't followed, yet this Blue Light guy found Ricco's office. We're not takin' any more chances."

"Okay, that makes sense," Sammy said, a little relieved as he sat back for the ride.

+++

On a nearby rooftop, the invisible Blue Light turned to follow the car, with Robert watching through the periscope Med created. Yet instead of crossing the alley to the next building, he stopped before reaching the edge.

"Robert, should we not pursue?"

Remember Sammy said he was around the corner? Well, that means the car will be back in the area, because their final destination is actually nearby. We're going to wait and watch for the car when it comes back.

"That is a wonderful idea. How long do you think it will take?"

Are you getting impatient Med?

"No, but my scans of you show growing fatigue. You did not acquire a complete rest before those men came to shoot you. Some of your internal chemicals are at elevated levels and–"

I get it. Okay, we'll wait for the car and the men to come and show us

Robert started getting a little nervous.

where they work out of, then I'll go home to rest. Ackers was tired. *You should probably recharge too. We'll get them tomorrow. Besides, it might be too much of a coincidence for Blue Light to show up again tonight.*

"I like that plan, but it is actually less than two hours before dawn now."

Really? Robert asked in disbelief. The hours had flown by.

"Is that not the vehicle in question?"

Yes, Ackers replied, seeing it drive back toward them on a back street. *We need to get to the next block and I want to see where they enter whatever building they're headed for. Help me down off this roof and we can go through that backyard and alley over there.*

"Understood."

+++

Still unseen, Blue Light landed in the backyard of the building and walked through the alley. Upon seeing the driver and Sammy get out of the car, he watched them walk into an apartment building.

We better make sure that this is actually their headquarters and not just another hideout that can be evacuated at a moment's notice.

"Agreed," replied Med.

The unseen figure moved up to the building's side but, uncertain how many might be within, remained outside. Robert was not up to another fight, so he asked Med to do his audio spying again.

Med extruded a thin, unseen filament into a warped window front that wasn't quite shut.

They heard a voice ask, "Where's Beta?"

"In the next room. He's waitin' for yah," someone answered.

Med moved the line around the wall to follow the footsteps and light knocking.

"Can I come in?" they heard Sammy ask.

A different voice responded. "Yes. What happened at Ricco's?"

"As I told Booker on the phone," Sammy began, "Blue Light crashed into Ricco's office. We were talking about that Ackers situation that Ricco sent a few guys out to resolve when we heard a rumble start in the outer office. Under the door we saw a flash of blue light, then gunshots and screaming. Then nothing. Next thing we knew, the inner office door smashed to splinters and the Blue Light guy is there. Ricco brought up a Tommy and shot the full box at the Light."

"So the Blue Light was hit. How badly?"

"Beat him back a bit but never knocked him down."

The other man sounded skeptical with an acerbic edge. "Had Ricco been sampling his wares and simply missed?"

"Not Ricco, he's always prepared. Blue Light just wasn't hurt at all. All the slugs went into him—it—and just stopped." Sammy's voice sounded awed. "Then they all fell out and dropped to the floor. Blue Light just stood there as if nothing happened. Then Ricco flipped out a switchblade and rushed him. His blade stuck in the light like the bullets. Blue Light just smacked him into the wall. That knocked him out. At that point I didn't stick around because I figured you'd want a report."

No sounds were heard for several moments.

"Robert, do you recognize that voice?" Med asked.

No. Should I?

"I am uncertain. Of course, when you have me within your pocket, my monitoring functions are not as accurate as they currently are."

It was then the other voice said, "I see. This is bad Sammy. Do we know any way to hurt this— thing?"

Sammy was silent for a bit before saying, "Maybe. Remember when he saved the family from the truck crash?"

"Yes," Beta admitted. "The report said he changed his body somehow, and that he was strong. The heat of the fire didn't bother him. How does that help us?"

"Well, when the truck and car exploded, the driver said that Blue Light was thrown some distance and then his light dimmed. It took a bit before becoming fully bright again. I also saw it dim just a little when Ricco opened fire on it. So maybe it can be slowed down if we throw enough firepower at it."

"I see what you're getting at," commented Beta, sounding intrigued. "Yes, that could mean an explosion might weaken him. So multiple blasts at the same time could do some actual harm. Maybe even kill it permanently. So we need to set something up. Okay, Sammy, you did the right thing. Now get going. I have some thinking to do."

Robert and Med heard Sammy leave the room and a few minutes later they saw him walk down the steps out of the building.

"I do not like the sound of that," said Med.

Neither do I. From now on, I want you to be as fully charged as possible at all times.

"Understood. Do we follow him Robert?" Med asked.

No. As you pointed out earlier, I'm tired. Let's go home. We have some planning of our own to do. They're gonna come up with a trap of some kind.

We must be ready for that.
"I will guide us back to your apartment."

CHAPTER 13

The walk back seemed to take forever. As they neared the apartment building, two things were quite apparent.

The sun was starting to rise over the horizon and a police car was parked at the curb out front.

Med, we better find a place where you can uncloak me. I need to be seen when I walk up.

"That alley over there has no one nearby or inside."

Works for me. When we get back out there, I'll likely be questioned. Let me handle it my way.

"Understood Robert."

If anyone had been paying attention, they would have noticed Robert Ackers suddenly appearing as if from nowhere. While he pretended to look puzzled at seeing a police car parked in his neighborhood, he continued onward as if it had nothing to do with him. It was only when he started walking up the front stairs that an officer stepped out from the passenger side of the unit and called out, "Mr. Ackers?"

Robert turned around to face the man. "Yes? What can I do for you officer?"

"Mind if I ask where you've been?"

"Well no, but what makes you ask?"

"There's been a problem in the building. In your apartment."

"My apartment?" Robert looked around as if in shock. "I don't see any signs of a fire. What happened?"

"You really don't know sir? Where have you been all night?"

"Look, I'm not sure whether or not you've heard about them, but after two separate incidents with criminals yesterday, I was a bit rattled, so I couldn't sleep last night. I finally went out for a walk to clear my head. So what happened to my place?"

"We can go up and you'll see. You're very lucky you weren't inside," the officer commented dryly.

The pair walked up the interior stairs to the second floor. Robert reacted appropriately on seeing the missing door and another police officer standing off to the side, watching it.

"Oh no!" Ackers exclaimed and went to move forward but the officer on duty barred his way as the one with him put a hand on his shoulder to stop him.

The door guard said, "Hi Sarge. Is this Ackers?"

The Sergeant replied, "Yes, he's just coming back from a walk."

"Lucky for him, those two were gunning for him."

Robert turned to the Sergeant and said, "Two men were WHAT?"

"They came to kill you Mister Ackers."

Robert's eyes opened wide in surprise and he croaked, "Coming to kill me? Why would they want to do that?" He looked around and asked, "Where are they? Did you guys get them?"

"Settle down," the Sergeant said. "Yes, we have them in custody. They've been arrested and are in jail at the precinct. But *we* didn't capture them."

"Oh, that's good, because I— Wait a minute! What do you mean *you* didn't capture them?"

"We were called to the scene. They were left here, bound and unconscious when we came in."

"Bound? By who? What happened here?" Robert was really playing his part, making himself sound like one of the innocent characters in his stories.

"Well, your neighbor across the hall said a big blue light did it."

"A blue light? Geez, Captain Rogen asked me about a blue light yesterday, and I told him what little I could then. How did this Blue Light capture the men who came to kill me?" Ackers was really getting into his role now.

The Sergeant took a deep breath and let out a sigh before answering. "The Blue Light was reported to be man shaped and quite large, about seven feet tall. Apparently he or it is very strong. He bound the gunmen in some heavy metal rods or something borrowed from a neighbor. Took us some time to remove them."

"I can't believe all this happened." Robert looked at the open doorway with the officer standing to the side. "That officer isn't going to be standing there forever, is he? Do you think some more people are coming to kill me?"

"No we don't," replied the Sergeant. "From what little we've been able to get from those two, they were sent with a spotter, who left before we got here. And we spoke to your landlady. What was her name?" He turned to the other officer.

"Mrs. Mondella," the door guard said before Robert could.

"Yeah, that's right. Mrs. Mondella says she'll have someone replace the door later today."

"She asked if we knew where she could find this Blue Light guy. She wants to chew him out and then have him reimburse her for the cost of the door," the guard added with a hint of a smile.

Robert simply nodded, though he wanted to smile too. "Yeah, I can believe that. She would, too. She's practically a force of nature."

The Sergeant rubbed his neck. "She is that. I wouldn't want to get on her bad side."

"So, what happens now?" Robert asked them.

"Well, I can leave the officer here until the door is fixed, but you have to promise me something."

"What's that Sergeant?"

"Get some sleep while you can because the captain wants to see you as early as possible."

"He wants to see me again? Why? I was the victim here," Robert said, pointing at the open door.

The Sergeant shrugged. "Just make sure you show up, okay?" He patted Ackers' shoulder and stepped back.

Robert walked into his apartment, and over his shoulder said, "Okay. Just let me clean up some and grab a quick nap. I'll come by after the new door is installed."

The Sergeant smiled and said, "Good." But before he walked away, he turned back and asked, "Where did you go last night?"

"What? Oh. just walked around downtown. Stopped at an all night diner for a cup of coffee. I just couldn't sit in here fretting."

"Good thing you didn't," the Sergeant said before walking away.

+++

Inside, Ackers went to his bedroom and closed the door.

Jeepers Med, I could really use some sleep now, but we should've expected this.

"*Expected what, exactly?*"

The police coming to interrogate me after my neighbor Oscar called them. Do you think I have time for a nap? I'm dragging right now.

"*Perhaps a short one. I can make it restful for you. You did tell the officers you would be in once the new door is installed, but we do not know when that will be. Besides, there is a mess in your main room to clean.*"

Mostly door pieces though. Let the workmen take care of that. Thankfully none of my personal belonging are damaged. Especially my typewriter!

"Would it seem strange if you did not clean?" Med asked.

Not as tired as I am. They figure this entire thing has been a shock to me. After kicking off his shoes, Ackers laid down on the bed with a sigh of relief. But he still tossed and turned, unable to get settled.

"Robert, you are not sleeping. Do we need to discuss something?"

Like what Med?

"That story you told the Sergeant. What if he tries to confirm it?"

Already have that covered. You've never been downtown in the heart of the city. There are always people out and about. I'm more concerned about what else the police are going to ask me.

"Because of this Captain Rogen?"

Partly. I don't know what his problem is, but it's unusual for a witness to be directly questioned by a police Captain. This incident might have really gained his attention after the first two, and he already warned me to stay out of police business. And Blue Light and I are seen in too many places together as it is, which is why I had you erase my name from that hit list.

"I understand your concerns now," Med said. "In the future we should give more consideration to keeping Robert Ackers separate from Blue Light."

Robert agreed and then he began to relax enough to get some sleep.

+++

Somewhat refreshed by a couple hours of sleep, Robert had just about finished clearing the majority of the mess about eight that morning when the officer on guard duty let Mrs. Mondella inside.

Robert politely asked how she was, to which she started shaking a finger at him and said, "How am I? I was up half o' the night wit' all the police and fuss, and back up early having to call for someone to come give you a new door. I'm a tired and I'm a mad. That's how I am."

"I'm sorry Mrs. Mondella. I went out last night because I couldn't sleep, but I never expected anything like this."

His landlady just looked at him for a moment before saying, "Well, I'm just glad you were not here and di'n't get hurt. But do you know that blue fellah? He owes me for a new door."

Ackers shook his head. "I've never seen him, Mrs. Mondella but if I do, I'll pass on the message."

"Good. They promise me your new door at nine. I won't a charge you since dis isn't your fault, but if I see that blue guy... mio Dio, he will get a piece my mind!"

"Understood Mrs. Mondella," and with that she turned and left.

"Robert, you lied to your landlady," Med pointed out to him.

Well just another little fib to cover our secret identity. After all, I've never really seen Blue Light since I can't see myself.

"But what about your reflect–"

ENOUGH MED! Robert mentally commanded, interrupting him. "Officer?" he called out.

"Yes?" The man said from the hallway.

"I'm going to fix myself some breakfast while waiting for the new door. Would you like anything?"

"Just coffee, if it wouldn't be too much trouble," the officer replied with a yawn.

"You got it," promised Robert. *Might as well buy some favors with the police while I can.*

"Is that legal?" Med inquired.

Depends upon how I go about it and what I do with them when needed.

By the time the meal was done, two men arrived to install Ackers new door. Mrs. Mondella and the officer oversaw the work from the hallway while Robert sat in the main room of the apartment and watched.

When they were done, the landlady split the new keys between herself and Ackers before showing the men and the officer out of the building.

Your door is now replaced. Should we not leave now? Med asked

Robert answered, "Yeah. Let's go see what Captain Rogen wants."

CHAPTER 14

Robert was heading toward the precinct, both him and Med on the alert for any potential danger, when he spotted Sarah coming towards him.

His heart seemed to skip a beat as he stopped. Sarah looked up and smiled sweetly and he thought her blue eyes were brighter than Med at full power as she approached.

"I had a nice time last night Sarah. Can we do that again sometime soon?"

Sara quickly said, "I'd love to Robert. Right now I'm heading to work. Have you eaten yet?"

"Yes. Unfortunately I'm on my way to the precinct to talk with Captain Rogen."

Sarah's smile turned into a frown as her eyes darkened. "Again? Has this anything to do with the purse snatcher or the diner robbery?"

Robert fidgeted as one of his feet swept the sidewalk in a nervous tic. "Uh, no. Something else came up."

"Let me guess. You captured another crook."

Robert shook his head. "No, nothing like that. Just, uh, something else happened, that's all."

Sarah's frown deepened and her voice turned arctic. "What exactly happened?"

There was no way he could avoid telling her now because if she found out otherwise, that would end things between them. So Robert was a vague as he could be about the details.

"Some guys broke into my apartment while I wasn't there. Look, Sarah I'll explain in more detail when I have the time, but right now I've really got to go. I'll see you later, okay."

"Yeah, okay, but then I'll want a full explanation," she told him with a questioning look before they parted company.

"Robert, you lied to her again," Med said, as Robert reluctantly walked away. *"You were–"*

Blue Light was there, not Robert Ackers.

"But you ARE Blue Light."

Yes, but even you said we need to think of Robert Ackers and Blue Light as two separate beings. That's how I want everyone else to think of them too.

The Medallion remained silent during the remainder of Ackers' trip to the police precinct.

Walking into the building, the desk sergeant recognized him immediately. "Ah, Mr. Ackers," the man said with a smile. "The captain is waiting for you in his office."

"Thank you Sergeant," Robert said, before walking over and knocking on the captain's door.

He entered at the invitation of, "Come in."

Captain Rogen looked up from his paperwork and said, "Good morning Mr. Ackers. Hope you finally slept." It was Rogen's way of letting him know his officers reported everything.

Ackers smiled slightly. "A brief nap but even under the circumstances, yes. I was pretty tired."

Rogen nodded. "Quite understandable. I gather you were fully informed about what happened? How fortunate for you that you weren't home at the time those armed men broke in."

"I can't argue with that!" Ackers began to sweat a bit. Rogen was a wily one. He knew how to interrogate someone in a way that might lead to a conflicting answer that would be further questioned. The Captain sat back with pursed lips and interlaced his fingers.

"So why exactly did you go out last night?" Rogen asked him in a flat tone. "Your landlady said you came home as did a couple of the other tenants."

Ackers stuck to his story.

"I did, and I was home for a while. But I just could not settle down after all that had happened during the day. I wasn't expecting anything like what the Sergeant told me, but part of my mind was wondering if any bad guys who got away would find out where I live and come beat me up or something like that. So I went out and headed downtown and just wandered around until I got tired enough to feel like going home. Then I get there and find out someone *did* come after me with the idea of killing me outright. So now I'm scared!" That part was certainly true and even the man across from him nodded, his stern look softening a bit. "So Captain Rogen, have you been able to find out anything from the men you captured?"

"*We* didn't capture them. We arrested them after Blue Light did the capturing," Rogen clarified.

"Blue Light? Wow, that guy has been all over the place lately."

"Guy?" Rogen said with an edgy tone. "I never said Blue Light was a man. Why would you say that?"

"I just assumed," Robert replied quickly, and his stomach began to churn a bit. This cop was good. Ackers shrugged and added, "The way you were talking about it just implied some man in costume maybe—"

Rogen snorted in derision."Frankly Mr. Ackers—say, may I call you Robert now that we've gotten to know each other so well?" At Ackers' abrupt nod he went on. "Robert, we don't understand what it is we're dealing with here. It could be a he, she, or it."

Ackers raised an eyebrow in feigned surprise as Rogen continued. "We only know that something that calls itself Blue Light, that glows and has a roughly human shape but can do amazing things, has been very active lately. So far it has been for the good of the people. If it continues I hope it remains that way. Truthfully though, I wish Blue Light wouldn't interfere in police business."

"Why not?" asked Robert, his hands outspread. "From what you've told me so far, this being has done nothing but good for the community."

Rogen frowned. "Yes, well, he's actually interfering and it makes the police department look incapable. That sends the wrong message to those who commit these crimes."

Robert matched the captain's frown, because he hadn't thought of that. "Oh, I see. Well, technically Robin Hood was in the same situation, but the only people truly against him were the King and the Sheriff of Nottingham."

Rogen frowned deeper. "Robin Hood was a legend in an old story. I fail to see how that compares to what we have on hand here and now."

Ackers had to concede him that. "Well sir, the officer at my broken door told me you wanted to see me so I'm here. Is that all you needed to know?" he asked, hoping to end this probing session quickly.

Rogen smiled like the cat who caught the canary. "Pretty much, although it's interesting that you and this Blue Light character have stopped crimes within a small amount of time. You've both done almost more work than any two cops in my precinct. Both of you somehow seemed to be involved in several important cases. It's almost like you are two sides of the same coin."

Well there it was. This man was catching on all too well!

"Robert, does he know about us?" Med asked with great concern.

No Med. He's fishing. Hoping I will make a mistake and admit something.

"He's a very astute person. What will you do?"

Ackers never got the chance to respond to Med as Rogen sat forward and caught his eye in a stern gaze, and asked the question he'd been dreading, "Robert Ackers, are you and Blue Light the same person?"

That bald-faced query caught him by surprise, but thinking quickly, Ackers turned his agitation into indignation. "You've got to be kidding! Seriously Captain, I was far away from my apartment when Blue Light was seen. I'd say it was sheer coincidence we've both been involved in the same situations in such a short time period because a lot of crime happens in my area these days.

"I mean, look at me—I'm no hero type," Robert added, arms outspread while glancing down at himself as in disbelief, but really to break the raptor-like gaze Rogen held on him. "I'm just a writer. I never wanted to be involved in any of this. I promise you I will try to stay away from any crimes or violence but I sure hope they stay away from me from now on too."

"I see," said Rogen, studying him with an expressionless gaze. "Well, thank you for your time. I appreciate you coming down promptly. Yet before you leave, can I show you something?"

"Sure," Ackers said cautiously. "If it's important."

Rogen let a little smile play around his lips. "It is. Come with me."

"Robert..."

Do not do anything unless I say otherwise, Ackers warned Med.

Rogen rose and waited for Robert, leading him down a flight of stairs into a room with what looked like a glass window on one wall. Peering into another room, Ackers saw one man sitting handcuffed at a table, a chain attached to an eye bolt keeping him tethered in place like a junkyard dog. The prisoner was facing a detective who had been questioning him. The handcuffed man never looked up at them and Robert realized he was peering through a one way mirror, something he had heard of but never seen before.

Rogen motioned Ackers to silence and then reached over and flipped a switch on a box next to the mirror. It activated an intercom system which allowed them to hear what was being said inside.

"C'mon Ricco," the detective prodded. "We have all kinds of documents detailing your criminal actions. Why don't you come clean? Tell us what you were doing, and why you sent men to kill Robert Ackers? What is he to you anyway?"

"I ain't saying nothing. Where's my lawyer?" Ricco demanded.

At that moment, from the hallway door that led into the interrogation room, everyone inside saw a blue light shine underneath the bottom edge of the door.

"Robert!"

Do not interfere Med!

Ricco's face blanched. The suspect started sweating profusely as he frantically tried to move away from the table he was attached to. "You can't do this to me! What's he doing here? Keep him away! Don't let him in! He's a monster! Nothing can hurt him! KEEP HIM AWAY!"

The detective turned toward the door and said, "Oh, I didn't know he was here. I don't think we can stop him from coming in if he wants to." Then he faced Ricco again, who was still trying to back away from the table and the door, a look of panicked hysteria in his bulging eyes and his arms stretched out the max in the chained cuffs.

"Do you still want to wait for your lawyer, Ricco?"

Ricco, yanking fruitlessly at the chain that kept him tethered to his side of the table, protested, "No, no! Just keep him away! I'll talk! Just keep him away!"

The detective walked over and knocked on the door. With that, the blue light receded and disappeared. Rogen shut off the intercom.

In the viewing room, Robert turned to Rogen and said, "I didn't know you had Blue Light here. So, is he one of your officers?"

Rogen's answer was to lead Ackers back into the hallway, where another officer stood with a flashlight in his hands. One brief push of the button showed the lens had been covered by a blue filter.

"Oh, now I see. You tricked him. Very clever Captain."

Rogen smiled. "Yes, I thought that might loosen Ricco's tongue."

"You know, even your prisoner referred to the Blue Light as a guy," Ackers pointed out, hoping to sway Rogen's opinion in his favor.

"True, but from eyewitness reports, it's hard to say officially what we're dealing with, between the weird voice and the bright blue light," Rogen replied in return.

Ackers shrugged. "Truthfully, I never really gave it much thought. Just glad he's helping to fight crime. There's so much of it out there now."

Rogen smiled, a little more warmly. "Want to see more of the interrogation?"

"Sure, if you don't mind." Robert Ackers also wanted to figure out where Captain Rogen was going with this part of having him come downtown for another 'talk'.

Rogen led Robert back into the viewing room and flipped the intercom back on.

They heard the detective say, "So, Ricco. We know all of the rackets you're involved in. The papers we found will convict you. But this latest caper just doesn't make sense. Why did you send those killers after Ackers?"

Ricco, still staring at the door, said, "He uh... he uh... he got in the way of two of the jobs I needed done. Got one of my guys pinched for the purse snatching and another robbing that diner. When I found out he had something to do with it, there's other people who don't like that kind of do-gooder. I had to send a message so no one else would do the same thing. It reflects bad on me, you see."

"So you've got someone else pulling your strings now. You want to tell me who that is?"

"I can't, because I don't know. But they'll make sure I don't talk to no one after this." Ricco continued staring at the door, but slouched in relief that the Blue Light did not return. Then he looked at the detective. "If

I squeal, someone offs me. If I don't, that thing out there takes me out. Either way I die."

"We can offer you police protection," the detective said in a reassuring tone.

"Not from the people I work for now, and not from that thing out there. I'm as good as dead."

"Then you might as well spill it. Otherwise I'll have someone else far less patient come in and take your statement."

"You won't let him in, will yah?" Ricco asked in a worried tone. "Promise me it won't be him!"

The detective smiled. "No Ricco. You're safe from him. For now. As long as you play it straight with us."

"Okay, I will!" promised Ricco.

With that Rogen turned off the speaker box and they left the room.

"That was clever Captain, using the Blue Light to get him to speak up," Ackers admitted, complimenting the man.

"Thank you Robert. Now you know why you should leave policing to the police. You don't want to endanger yourself or anyone else. Especially not the young woman you were here with before. These mobsters play for keeps and have no mercy."

"No, I wouldn't want that," said Ackers, concerned for Sarah now. "I'll do my best to keep out of your hair."

"Good. Thank you for coming down. Oh, and if you see Blue Light, please ask him to come by too. I have a few questions for him. I promise I won't try to arrest or detain him. Not that I think I could," Rogen added as an afterthought with just the hint of a smirk.

"Anytime Captain. But if you see him first, please tell this Blue Light that Mrs. Mondella says he owes her for the cost of replacing my door."

That made Captain Rogen pause. "Mrs. Mondella— She's your landlady, right?"

"Yes. Do you know her?" Ackers asked.

"Only from the reports of her husband being killed." Rogen looked thoughtful. "I'll have someone take a closer look over Ricco's papers. I'm sure there's a lot more we can ask him about."

"You think he may have had something to do with that?" Robert asked. "If so, I'm sure Mrs. Mondella would like to know, and she'd be relieved that you got her husband's killer." He was recalling the tough that tried shaking her down for money.

"We'll find out," promised Rogen. "I don't like open cases but until we do know, it's probably best you don't say anything to her."

"Understood."

"Thank you Robert. Have a quiet day now."

With that, Ackers was free to leave.

+++

It was not until they were out of the precinct headquarters and on the way back to Ackers' apartment when Med asked, *"Robert, does this mean Captain Rogen knows you are Blue Light?"*

I don't think he knows for sure, Med, Robert mentally replied. *I do think he suspects something between the two, but has no proof. We'll need to be more careful when we do anything as Blue Light. We don't want any additional scrutiny, so I'll try not to get involved in any crime stopping while I'm not Blue Light.*

"How will you manage that if these criminals keep coming after you?"

I don't know. I'll do what I have to. Wow, it's almost noon, Roberts added, glancing at his watch. *I could use a sandwich.*

"Are we going to Sarah's diner for your sustenance?"

I guess so. It's on the way home, and though I would rather not face Sarah, I need to talk to her. I'm sure she won't be pleased when she finds out about what happened last night in the apartment. The police didn't question me about my alibi but I'm pretty sure she will.

"Can you just lie to her?" asked Med. *"You have already done so several times today, so I know you do not have any issues with it."*

Yeah, well, I don't like lying, but I have to protect our identities. But I really like Sarah and she likes me too, so I need to be truthful with her when and where I can be. If she catches me in a lie, it will be worse than telling the truth.

"Should you try to avoid her?"

Robert sighed and answered, *No. That will just make things worse. Better to face it now.*

"You are probably correct in your assessment," agreed Med, *"but I do have one question. How did Captain Rogen know about Sarah?"*

That had bothered Ackers too. *I don't know. From the police report? From one of the officers we've already encountered? It's not like I'm hiding her or anything.*

Med had no reply as they finished walking to the diner.

CHAPTER 15

As Robert entered the diner, Diana the cashier smiled and greeted him. "Mr. Ackers, I have a booth empty in Sarah's zone. She'll be out of the kitchen to take care of you in a minute."

Robert saw the cashier pointing to a sunny spot near a window and replied, "Thanks, but I think I'll sit somewhere else today."

"Oh—is something wrong?" She looked worried.

"No. Nothing like that. I'm just tired and don't want the sun in my eyes right now."

"Okay. Well, there's a booth in the back, away from the windows. But Mildred takes care of that one."

"That's fine. I'm sure Sarah will understand. See you later."

Ackers walked to the last booth, his back to the kitchen when Mildred, a middle aged woman with fading red hair and freckles, arrived.

"Hello sir. Would you like a menu?" she began her usual patter, until seeing who the customer was. "Oh, Mr. Ackers. Are you sure you don't want your usual booth so Sarah can take your order?"

"No, thank you Mildred. I'll have a hamburger—no, make that a cheeseburger, with lettuce, tomato, and onion. Medium rare, with fries and a soda."

Mildred wrote the order on her pad, keeping the menu tucked under her elbow against her side. "Right you are. Be back in a few minutes."

"Robert, when will you tell Sarah about what happened last night?" Med asked. *"She will be sure to inquire as to why you had to see Captain Rogen again and she does seem to care about you."*

Ackers sighed while mentally replying, *I know Med. I just want a little time to figure out how to tell her. I have a feeling she'll be upset with me when she finds out, so if I let some time pass before we speak, maybe she won't be as angry.*

"I do not think that strategy will work."

Huh? Why?

"The waitress who took your food order must have told Sarah you were here, for she is walking this way."

Damn!

Sarah sat down in the booth across from Robert, with a confused look on her face. "Did you think I wouldn't know you were here? Are you trying to hide from me?"

Robert shook his head and said, "Of course not Sarah. I just didn't want the sun in my eyes, which it would have been in the other booth. How are you? You look great, as usual."

"Fine, but don't try to distract me. I want to know why were you meeting with Captain Rogen again. Did something happen last night?"

Sarah would make a good detective. Sighing, Robert's shoulders slumped in resignation before he told her. "Okay, I owe you an explanation. Last night while I was still out, a couple of mugs broke in. My door was broken and Mrs. Mondella had to replace it today."

"I see," Sarah said, looking directly at him. "So last night, after you dropped me off, you didn't go directly to your apartment, and when you did your door was broken by two men, who wanted to do what, exactly?"

"Um, well," Robert fingered his collar as if it was too tight. "Captain Rogen says they were there to, uh—" he leaned forward and whispered, "to kill me."

Sarah bolted up and slammed her fists on the booth's table surface while shouting, "THEY WERE THERE TO KILL YOU?"

The diner wasn't that busy but both staff and customers were turning and staring to see what the sudden hullabaloo was all about.

Robert gently placed a calming hand on her arm, flinching at all the people gawking at them. "Sarah, not so loud. You're making a scene," he requested in a low voice. "Please sit down. That's what Captain Rogen claims, but I don't know for sure. I do know those guys didn't get to do whatever they planned to because I wasn't there." *Quiet Med, let me handle this my way,* he warned silently as his unseen partner began to correct him. "I was kind of wound up after our date—in a good way," he added with a smile and she gave him a brief thin smile, so he went on. "So I went for a walk. People at my building claim that Blue Light character took care of the guys who broke in, so I'm only out a front door."

He made it sound simple, not wanting to worry Sarah any more than she already was. "Anyway, speaking of our date. I *really* enjoyed myself last night," he added, smiling broadly. "Can we do it again tonight?"

"Someone tried to kill you last night and you want me to go out with you tonight?" Sarah asked in disbelief. "Are you nuts?"

"Just about you Sarah. You're the best thing that has ever happened to me," Robert said with feeling, still holding her hand. *Well, second greatest,* he mentally told Med. "Besides, the guy who ordered the hit on me is in custody and he's not likely to get out anytime soon. So, I'm safe right now.

Captain Rogen said so."

"*Robert, Rogen said no such thing,*" Med pointed out as Sarah simply stared at him, her warring emotions evident in her eyes.

Finally, she said, "I'll think about it, but I really have to get back to work now." With that she left the booth.

"*Robert...*" Med began, the voice somewhat reproachful.

Look, Rogen said as much, since he had the guy who ordered the hit on me in custody.

"*But, what you told Sarah–*"

I told her what I had to so she'd calm down and not worry so much about being with me. I did what was necessary, nothing more.

"*I find you humans... somewhat confusing. Are all of you like this?*"

Med, humans are a unique combination of thinking, logic, emotions, and illogical thought. Considering you're a computing machine who isn't affected by emotions like us biological beings—and I still don't quite understand what that means—I'm not surprised you're confused.

"*Robert, why do you think I do not possess any feelings or emotions?*"

Robert considered how to respond to Med's question as Mildred returned with a plate of food and his soda. "Is there anything else I can get for you, Mr. Ackers?"

"No, thank you Mildred," he politely replied, getting ready to dig into the meal.

Mildred hung around for a moment before saying, "Mr. Ackers, this may be none of my business, but you do know Sarah likes you? She likes you a lot."

Robert looked up at the waitress and grinned. "Well, I like her a lot too."

"Well, she's in the back crying her eyes out right now. Were you really on a hit list?"

Robert abruptly lost interest in his food. "Unfortunately yes, but please don't spread it around. Can I go in the back? I'd really like to talk to Sarah."

"I'm not sure that would be the best thing at the moment. You might want to finish your meal first. Let her cry it out and wait for Sarah to compose herself," Mildred advised sagely.

He pushed his plate away, saying "Mildred I appreciate your advice, but I'm not hungry anymore. Could you have someone wrap this up to go? I think it would be best if I speak with her now."

Mildred just shrugged and said, "It's your funeral."

As the older waitress took his food away and went back to her duties, Robert rose and walked resolutely to the door to the diner's back room.

"THEY WERE THERE TO KILL YOU!"

Looking through the built-in window, he saw Sarah sitting on a bunch of boxes, sniffling and trying to dry her eyes with her apron.

Quietly entering the room, he sat down next to her and gently put an arm around her.

"I'm sorry," Robert began. "I didn't mean to make you cry. I promise I won't get involved in any crime stopping ever again."

Still sniffling, Sarah said, "I see Mildred has a big mouth. Oh Robert, I'm just so worried about you getting hurt. Or worse!" She turned and looked at him. "Look, one of the things I really like about you is your sense of right and wrong. So don't change that. You say you won't ever get involved, but I know better, because it's a part of you. It's who and what you are."

"Robert, maybe we should stop the actions we have been taking as Blue Light for a while," suggested Med. *"It makes Sarah uneasy, and she is important to you. I do not fully comprehend these human emotions, but her mood seems to be upsetting you as well."*

Not now Med! Please stop monitoring everything while I'm with Sarah. Ackers turned his attention back to the woman beside him as Med shut down its constant surveillance.

"Sarah, what do you want me to do?" Robert asked, staring directly into her eyes. "I'm a writer and when I'm writing nothing happens to me, only to my characters. But when I see something bad happening, like the diner robbery attempt, I just can't stand around and do nothing. Would you still like me if I did that?"

Sarah looked down. "No, I really like you as you are. I think I did the first day you came into the diner," she admitted, turning to face him. "But you're not a policeman and you don't have a dangerous job and yet you seem to put yourself into harmful situations, and now someone sent men to— To kill you!" Her voice trailed off as the tears began to flow again.

He tried to be reassuring. "Yes, but all of those people are in jail now. They can't hurt me anymore."

"Only if they stay there," she snapped. "Suppose they get out on bail or escape?"

He'd thought of that too, but Blue Light could handle it. He just couldn't tell Sarah that—at least not right now.

"Captain Rogen interrogated them and they confessed. I don't think they're getting out anytime soon. Does that make you feel better?"

Sarah sniffed and dried her eyes with the apron again, before staring at Robert with pleading eyes. "Yes, a little, but—"

"Sarah, do you think your boss will let you get out early? I'd like to take a walk with you. Also, I think I have my appetite back, and I'm sure the burger I left out there is cold. Let me take you out to eat. Anyplace you want."

"Well, let me ask if I can leave early. I haven't really worked much today."

Fortunately Sarah's boss was understanding, for she had been very shaken up by the recent robbery attempt. A few minutes later Robert and Sarah walked out of the diner, side by side though not holding hands.

"So, where would you like to have lunch?" Robert asked. "Afterward we could go to the park, or a movie, or— Well, whatever you want."

Sarah smiled and began considering the possibilities when they were interrupted by a police officer approaching them.

"Hello Mr. Ackers," said Officer Hadley. "Broken up any more robberies today?" he asked in jest, not seeing the frown on Sarah's face, which had gone pale again. Hadley quickly tipped his hat and said, "How-do Miss."

Embarrassed, Robert looked first at Sarah, then Hadley. "No officer. We were just going out for lunch. Any suggestions?"

"I see. Well, there's the German place two blocks down. They have excellent strudel. Then there's the Chinese. I love their Chow Mein. Then there's Giuseppe's on First Avenue. Terrific chicken Parmesan and pasta. Unfortunately they're the most expensive, but it's a really good eat."

Sarah looked up and smiled at Robert. "I love Italian, but not if they're so expensive."

"That sounds fantastic. Don't worry about the expense right now. I've still got money left from selling my last story though maybe next time we'll get some spaghetti and meatballs. Mrs. Mondella makes it terrific," Robert bragged.

"Mrs. Mondella? Isn't she your landlady?" Sarah asked.

"Yeah, she owes me a dinner because... um, never mind. So, what's the name of the Italian place again?" Ackers asked Hadley.

CHAPTER 16

After a hearty afternoon meal, Robert and Sarah went for a long walk in the park. They talked about anything and everything that came to mind, except for the situation that caused the trouble between them in the first place.

Robert feared that problem would remain unresolved at least for the foreseeable future, but preferred a happy girlfriend to a worried one. As the sun was setting, they shared a final kiss at the steps to her apartment building, then reluctantly parted company for the night. Robert went home.

His other companion had been strangely silent throughout the afternoon. Whether out of respect or trying to process everything was unknown. Yet he was a bit startled to hear Med mentally speak now.

"Robert, I have remained dormant as requested. May we speak now?"

Sure Med. Look, I'm sorry about the misunderstanding between us, but when it comes to Sarah, I need to handle my relationship with her my own way.

"Yes, I can see you are very happy. There are certain chemicals that have heightened in your brain. You had an enjoyable outing with Sarah?"

Oh, yeah. Did you hear what she said in the diner? She liked me on first sight! That's pretty amazing to hear. Now, all I need to do is stay clear of problems when I'm out in the world as myself. Especially when I'm with her.

"Does that mean we will not be going out tonight to investigate?"

Well, Robert Ackers won't, but Blue Light certainly will.

+++

That Med had kept silent and not actively monitored Robert's surroundings worked well in the favor of someone who had followed them from the diner. The person stayed out of sight as they spoke with Officer Hadley, and only dawdled nearby as they ate at the Italian restaurant and then walked in the park. The surreptitious watcher followed them back to the area of Sarah's apartment building, lingering long enough for Ackers to head home and the girl to go inside. Then it left and caught a cab uptown.

This was information that would be paid for. Something that would likely bail the boss out when his superiors got wind of it. That do-gooder Ackers was becoming a nuisance and it had already been noted that wherever he went, Blue Light was never too far off. While the actual connection was uncertain, obviously the best way to flush that luminous hero out in the open would be to get to Ackers first. And to do that, they needed more than just guns, knives, and knuckle-dusters.

They needed bait.

+++

Later that moonless night the stars shone brightly against their nocturnal black velvety background. The sparse and barely maintained street lights were swallowed up in the gloom and scarcely illuminated their targeted areas. Far from the neon lit downtown heart of the city; this older district was in one of the more unsavory areas. It had a bad reputation and so most people avoided it, even in daytime.

In front of a previously visited building, a windblown newspaper seemed to strike something and stay suspended in midair for a moment with no visible means of support before departing in a different direction, as if brushed off.

Med, let's see if anyone—especially some new gang boss—is in, an invisible Blue Light mentally said to his artificially intelligent companion.

"As you wish Robert. I am sending in a filament that will allow us both to hear anything inside."

The unseen, wire thin tendril slid in under the front door into a first floor apartment.

At first there was nothing to hear but the occasional rustle of papers, then a voice asked, "Sammy, what have you heard about Ricco and the others who got pinched?"

Another voice Robert recognized replied, "Well, according to our snitch in the precinct, Ricco's been squealing. A lot. Seems the cops tricked him, although the fink doesn't know how. They got Ricco more terrified of whatever they threatened him with than he is of us."

"Ricco knows what will happen if he squeals, so what could the cops have done to him?" the other voice asked.

"No idea," admitted Sammy. "Worse, they got all his papers too."

"Damn him! I told him not to keep records of his work. What else did they get? Has he mentioned me?"

"No. At least not yet," Sammy replied. "And them two hired trigger men have been talking too, though our insider says Ricco is taking all the heat from them. They didn't know about you, so they can't say anything to get you in Dutch."

"Good. We'll have to take care of Ricco as soon as possible," the other voice said in a callous tone. "What have you found out about this Blue Light?"

"Not a thing," confessed Sammy. "The police don't know who he is or where he came from, and none of our people on the street do either. The only things we know about him are what that truck driver told Ricco, and the reports from some bystanders at the car crash and the bank."

"So, get the truck driver here and let's ask some more questions."

"Too late for that, he's a stiff now. Ricco put some daylight in him after finding out about the accident. Ricco was livid about losing forty grand worth of China White and Weed."

The other man sighed. "Damn Ricco, always does his convincing with his gat. So sum up what we do know about Blue Light."

"He's big, strong, and seems able to change his shape," began Sammy. "He shines blue, hence the name. Oh yeah. When the cars exploded he was thrown some ways and his light dimmed a bit. After a few seconds it came back full."

"Nothing new there. Anything else?"

"Well, at the bank robbery, one of the guys hit him with a sledgehammer. It seemed to have an effect, briefly. Then there's Ricco's attack on him. Blue Light seemed to— I don't know, catch all the slugs Ricco pumped into him without too much effect. But the boss' shiv seemed to get into the Light. Didn't cut him, but still made an impression."

"Go on," ordered the other voice.

"The attack on the Leventhals, well there the guns had no affect. I think that was the first time he appeared. I have no reports on him before that."

"I see. It seems like explosions can hurt him and sharp objects or hard knocks from behind are somewhat effective," the questioner mused. There was silence for over a full minute before he spoke again. "We need to set up a situation for Mr. Blue Light. Something he can't resist getting involved in. He seems to like helping people. Let me think on this. Meanwhile, Spats, I need some things,"

A third voice asked, "What kinda things?" Ackers was irritated that they never seemed to mention this man's name or rank in the gang.

"I'll make a list and give it to you when I'm ready. Now both of you get out and let me think."

The other two voices receded, before Robert and Med heard footsteps and a door closing.

It was quiet for a moment before the man said out loud, "Mr. Blue Light, you're going to be in for a real surprise. You now have the interest of very important people who play for keeps."

Then it grew quiet.

+++

"*Robert, are you going in there now to get him arrested like that Ricco person?*'

No. Ricco had incriminating evidence in his files. You saw that before we went in. We knew those files would keep him in jail for a long time. This guy is smarter than Ricco and I don't think he's part of this gang. Did you see any files in his office which would implicate him in any crimes?

"*No. But then I was focused on getting the audio transmissions you wanted.*"

Okay. Right now we need to either catch him in the act, or get his mobsters to turn against him. Like Ricco's hirelings did.

"*Do you have a plan?*"

Kinda, but he's also planning something and that worries me. Some way to trap or eliminate Blue Light. We need to be prepared for that.

"*How?*"

For now we go back home. I need to rest and do some writing. The past few days have been too busy for that, and I need to make money to pay the bills.

"*Is there no way to use your Blue Light persona to earn money? As long as we do not break any laws or regulations ourselves in the process, I would be willing to—*"

No. I don't want to make Blue Light into a mercenary—that's a warrior for hire. I can't think of any other way for Blue Light to earn money.

"*How about providing security services?*" asked Med. "*There were guards in the bank who were not police officers. Or Blue Light could become a police officer. They are paid for doing that work, are they not?*"

Frankly I don't like either idea. Blue Light is not a human being—or at least doesn't appear to be one. Both positions require training or experience and he'd never be accepted for that. And it's dangerous to be out there all the time. Plus adding on that sort of responsibility would take me away from my writing and I still enjoy that.

"*Captain Rogen pointed much of this out to you when you spoke to him,*" Med reminded Robert.

I know, but the police wouldn't be able to legally do some of the things we have done to capture the crooks. So we are helping them, even if they don't like the way things are done and nothing would hold up in court trials. That was a troubling thought.

Med picked up on Ackers' reasoning very quickly. The judicial system in his country required things to be done in a certain way and that even criminals had rights to a fair and impartial trial. "*Does that mean our work so far has been useless?"*

No, since we also made sure to have corroborating evidence to prove their guilt. So Blue Light continues as is: an unknown crime fighting champion of justice. Beside, our adventures might be something I could base some stories on, without revealing my existence. I'll need to think about that. But for now it's time to go home.

With that, Med retrieved his tendril and they left.

+++

Unfortunately Med and Robert Ackers left a little too soon. A few minutes later Spats reentered the office at his superior's request.

"I have that list of items I want you to get Spats," the new boss said, while handing him a sheet of paper.

The other man looked it over before commenting. "That's quite a list. You sure we need this much explosive and ammo?"

"Better too much than too little."

"Yeah, okay," Spats said, before asking, "A vacant lot? Any kind in particular?"

"Something fairly large. It doesn't need to be totally vacant. A new construction site would be good."

Spats nodded in acknowledgment. "It might take us a bit to acquire everything. How soon do you want it?"

The man he was speaking to smiled, thinking of some other information he was now privy to that should draw this Blue Light out in the open. "As soon as you can get your hands on it," he drawled and then got to his feet when he heard a vehicle pull up outside. "Our mutual benefactor wants this settled immediately. We have enough leverage now to move in on this mysterious do-gooder. Once Blue Light is history, it won't be long before we own this city. So don't disappoint us."

And then he took his leave, getting into the back seat of a long, dark, unmarked car that was awaiting him.

+++

While Robert and Med were clandestinely making their way home, Mrs. Mondella, in her dressing gown with her hair in rollers, opened the front door of her unit to find a policeman had been ringing her door bell.

"Mrs. Mondella? I'm Captain Rogen," he said, showing his badge to her.

"I command the precinct here. May I speak with you?"

Mrs. Mondella scrutinized him carefully, then said, "Yes. Come this way please."

She led him inside and gestured for him to sit at the kitchen table while she went in the small living room to shut off the radio station.

"Would you like a cuppa coffee? It's Italian. Won't take long to brew."

Rogen smiled briefly but shook his head. "Thank you Mrs. Mondella, but I won't be long. I'd like to talk to you about your husband."

She sat down and wiped her now sweating hands on her robe. "My husband? He was killed last year in his store," she reminded him, before using the collar of the robe to wipe some tears away.

"Yes, I know. It was a robbery gone bad, or so we thought at the time. Unfortunately we still haven't caught the robber, but we've come upon some more information."

She stared at him with red eyes. "What kinda info'mation?"

"We have the man who ordered your husband killed in custody and we know who the gunman is."

"WHAT?" Mrs. Mondella screamed. "He was ordered killed? Why? By who?"

"It's still an active investigation until we catch the killer, but it seems your husband refused to pay protection money. The man we have in custody ordered him killed to make an example of people who don't pay."

"Dat sounds like my Alphonso, but he never told me about no protection money." Then Mrs. Mondella was silent for a moment before asking, "Can I visit this bastardo?"

"That might not be a good idea. Better let the law handle it," Rogen advised her.

"Fine, as long as he gets what's coming to him for taking my Alphonso away from me," she replied, fighting the tears.

"He will—I'll personally see to that. Look, I'm sorry to upset you, but I thought you should know, and I didn't want to just send the local beat cop over to give you the news. I'll leave you now," said Rogen, not wanting to be around for more crying, "but I do want to warn you to be careful who you let into this building from now on. When we catch the killer, I'll inform you personally." He was about to get to his feet.

She nodded and drew a deep breath. "I thank you for comin' Captain Rogen, but if I can ask, how did you catch that bastardo?"

Rogen relaxed back into the seat, for this was what he really wanted to talk to her about. "The police didn't actually capture him. We arrested him after a report came in about some shooting at another apartment; not the incident here. There was criminal evidence lying around that gave us what we needed to arrest them."

"So who did capture these crooks?"

She was sharp! "The men we arrested kept talking about this Blue Light creature that has been in the news so much," Rogen answered, hoping bringing that up might lead to further conversation.

"The Blue Light?" Mrs. Mondella said in surprise. "He get the men who tried to kill one-a my renters. He owes me for a door I had to replace."

Having done interrogations before, Rogen played it cool. "Ah yes— As I recall, the renter was a Robert Ackers?"

"Yes, he's a nice young man. He help me when another mafioso come to demand money from me. Do you know Mister Ackers?"

Rogen smiled slightly. "We've met. Funny, I never saw a report on this attempted shakedown. Tell me Mrs. Mondella, when did this happen?"

"Last week." She shrugged. "No, mebbe two week ago. It don't matter, Mr. Ackers he scare the man away."

That was interesting, because Robert Ackers was far from powerful or scary. Yet he'd been involved to some extent in several such situations lately. Rogen thought about that while saying, "I see. Well thank you Mrs. Mondella. I promise we'll be in touch."

"Thank you for telling me dese things, Captain."

She let him out her door and locked it after him. Rogen walked outside to his waiting car, opened a door and sat in the back, deep in thought.

His driver gazed at him in the rear view mirror, then asked, "Where to now? Back to the precinct?"

It took Rogen a moment to realize he had been spoken to. "Yeah. Looks like an all-nighter for me. I need to do some research."

CHAPTER 17

After a decent night's sleep and the best breakfast he could fix for himself, Robert Ackers was at his typewriter creating another story when Med announced, *"Robert, there is someone at your door."*

The clackity-clack of the typewriter stopped as Ackers mentally asked, *Do you know who it is? Do they have guns?*

"No, but I believe the visitor is female, for the figure is much smaller than

any of the males that came to your door the other night."

Mrs. Mondella?

"No."

Then what woman would come to see me? Robert asked as there was a knock on the door.

"If you answer the door, you might find out."

Are you starting to get snarky with me?

"If I knew what that word meant, then I could properly respond to your query."

With a chuckle Robert went to the door and opened it to see—

"Sarah!" he exclaimed. "It's great to see you, but why aren't you working? What are you doing here?"

Sarah smiled at him. "I came to see you, silly. This is my day off and I thought we could go to the park and walk again. Maybe go to a movie like we didn't get to do the last time. May I come in?"

"Oh— sure, of course. Please," Robert said, a bit flustered while letting her enter.

Sarah looked around the simple room, then blushed upon seeing the rumpled bed through the open bedroom alcove. She turned to avoid thinking about that, then spotted the table with the typewriter and paper in the roller. "Did I interrupt your writing?"

"That's okay. I'm having a problem with part of the story anyway. Yet even if I didn't need a chance to clear my head, I'd love to go out with you. After the park we can see about a movie. The local house has a Clark Gable film. Would you like that?"

"That would be wonderful!" She sounded really enthusiastic and his heart skipped a beat.

"Let me get my jacket and we'll go."

"Robert, is this another part of the dating and mating ritual?"

Yes Med, and this actually takes it to another level since Sarah initiated it this time. It means we're getting closer.

"After this, then what is the next step? Mating?"

Not now Med!

Robert suddenly stopped in mid-step as Sarah looked at him questioningly. "Is something wrong?"

"Um, no," he replied. "For a moment I thought I forgot something, but it's okay. I'm ready to go."

As Robert put on his jacket and escorted Sarah back out, he thought, *Look Med, humans generally don't go to that step this quickly. If you have any other questions about relationships, please ask them later when we're alone.*

"Understood. I do find this ritual fascinating, but also somewhat prolonged. Why not just proceed to the final steps? Does the mating process always take this long?"

You have a lot to learn about people, but I want to take it slow because I'm hoping for a very long term relationship with Sarah. Save the rest of your questions for later, Ackers insisted firmly. *I want to give Sarah all of my attention.*

"Very well. I will simply observe."

We'll need to talk about that later, too.

+++

As Robert and Sarah walked back downstairs, Med never spoke up about Ackers' elevated vital signs when Sarah put her arm through his.

They were making small talk without a care in the world when Robert saw Mrs. Mondella in the entryway sweeping.

"Hello Mrs. Mondella. I'd like you to meet Sarah Baker."

"Is this the girl you meet at the diner? She's very pretty," the older woman said with a knowing smile.

"I think so too," agreed Robert, and heard Sarah's quickly indrawn breath as she leaned in a bit closer. "Sarah, this is Mrs. Mondella, my landlady."

Sarah smiled and said, "Pleased to meet you, and thank you for the compliment."

Mrs. Mondella turned to Robert and suggested, "She's a nice girl. Maybe you bring her by for that dinner I owe you?" Then she turned to Sarah and bragged, "I make the best spaghetti and meatballs. Besides, I owe him one."

Sarah looks puzzled. "You owe him a dinner? Why is that?" She could feel Robert going stiff beside her and that made Sarah even more curious.

"He help me with a ladro who come for money."

Sarah's face turned from friendly to a bit stern as she hesitantly asked, "What is ladro?"

"How you say? A thief. He chase him away, and he get a little hurt, but your Mister Ackers is molto coraggioso—very brave. He is a good young man." Mrs. Mondella obviously thought she was helping Robert by telling the story.

"I see. He chased off another thief—" Sarah repeated in an ominous monotone while turning to face a now uncomfortable Robert with a deep frown. "When was this Robert, and why didn't you tell me?"

"Hold on Sarah please," he begged. "All I did was yell at him and he ran off."

Which was when Mrs. Mondella added, "After he shoot you, yes."

"He shot you?" a shocked Sarah said in a rather loud voice. A nearby tenant peeked out and Mrs. Mondella waved him off.

"It was just a grazing shot, nothing serious. It happened about two weeks ago. I'm fine, really," Robert protested, while pointing at his head. "See? All healed. No scar."

Mrs. Mondella nodded in agreement and smiled. "I'm glad, because there was so much blood! Scare me half to death. Anyway, so maybe you two can come to dinnah tonight?" she asked, completely changing the subject.

"There was a lot of blood—" Sarah said in a sick tone. "You got shot, and there was a lot of blood. I don't like this Robert. You seem to be determined to play hero and get yourself killed." She huffed and crossed her arms. "I might need to think about going out with you."

Robert stared at her with a sad expression on his face. "Sarah, please. I couldn't let Mrs. Mondella face that guy alone. I wasn't seriously hurt and it's not like I planned any of this. I would really like to keep seeing you."

"I'm not sure," Sarah replied, turning away from him. "I don't go out with hooligans or troublemakers Mister Ackers. You seem to get involved in a lot of dangerous situations."

"But Sarah, I don't go looking for trouble."

"*Actually Robert...*" began Med.

Not now Med! Robert pleaded as he continued trying to convince Sarah everything was all right.

"Honestly Sarah, I'm really a pretty quiet guy. But if I do see someone who needs help, how can I just turn away and not get involved? After all, what would have happened at the diner if I wasn't there?" he asked, to which she had no immediate response. He could see the warring emotions in her blue eyes. "If it bothers you that much, I'll understand if you don't want to continue seeing me, though that would make me really sad. But I have to do what I think is right."

Sarah bit her lip and turned to face him. "Well, that is actually part of why I like you. Your willingness to help others. You have a kind heart Robert, which makes me feel you might be the right man for me, but please do try not to get into any more risky situations. Call the police and let them handle things."

Robert grinned broadly. "I'll do my best. Do you still want to go for that walk and a movie?"

Sarah smiled back at him. "Yes, I actually do," she answered, hooking her arm into his as they resumed heading out together.

Mrs. Mondella had stepped back to let them work things out between them. She watched them exiting the front door of the apartment building together, then called out, "Don't forget to come to dinnah tonight!"

+++

Someone who had been loitering outside the apartment building ducked around the corner when Robert and Sarah came out, and watched them pass by. The freckle faced young man in high waist, baggy trousers with suspenders over a less than clean white shirt let them get far enough ahead that he would not seem to be following them. Then settling his newsboy cap at a rakish angle, he fell in behind them at a distance, pretending to be causally strolling down the sidewalks while looking around at random buildings and trees.

They were headed for the park. That was a good place to be alone with a girl. Plenty of cover too. As long as he remained well behind and somewhat out of sight, the watcher would be able to get an idea of how close these two were getting now. The trick was to keep them in sight without being seen. You could tell a lot about someone just by the way they walked though, and they were taking their fat sweet time, strolling along and not saying too much until they got to the park gate. Once inside, they relaxed and began talking nonstop. Now and then the girl would giggle. All but the billing and cooing was going on. That likely came later, when they were alone.

Sammy would want to know that the dame from the diner actually came to see Ackers today, so these two were getting tight. This was something that could be easily exploited to bring that do-gooder to his knees and maybe smoke out his big blue buddy. Orders had come down from the uptown Big Shot who was running things now that Ackers was not to be molested until they could get a handle on this Blue Light character. Once they had a good idea of what it took to bring that glowing, interfering crusader out into the open, they'd reel Ackers in and set a trap.

In the meantime though, they now had a way to get Ackers' full cooperation. The girl was the key. If she was in any danger, that should make Ackers more protective of her. They had been told to issue a warning first, and if Ackers didn't take the bait, or if the Blue Light immediately showed up, the next time things would get a whole lot more serious.

The young man came across someone he knew would be waiting, and they had a quick and low-voiced conversation. Then he went on his way and the other man—older and far more ready to be drastic with his approach—began to stalk the two young lovers.

+++

Sarah and Robert had made their peace and walked into the park arm in arm before strolling down a landscaped path.

After the tense conversation earlier, each had remained mostly silent until Robert broke the ice between them. "It's a beautiful day for a walk. Especially with you."

Sarah leaned against him and smiled. "I do love the park and the weather is perfect. Listening to the birds singing in the trees makes me feel like I don't have a care in the world. I'm glad you thought of this."

"Me too. Do you want to sit on that bench?" Robert asked, seeing the one ahead was empty.

She agreed, noticing, "Oh look Robert! There are squirrels chasing each other around."

Perfect timing Mother Nature! They sat and quietly enjoyed the crazy antics of the squirrels, a passing butterfly, and each other's company.

Robert moved his arm tighter around Sarah's shoulders and she leaned further into him.

"I love the quiet times like this, especially sharing it with you, Sarah."

"So do I. I wish this day could last forever." She sounded so sincere that his heart pounded in his ears.

"Robert, what does Sarah mean? Do not humans have only a finite lifespan?"

Robert mentally sighed. *Yes Med. Our time on this earth is limited. What Sarah meant was she wished this moment never ended. If you want to ask me any further questions, please do it later. I'd like to enjoy this time with Sarah, WITHOUT COMMENTARY.*

Despite being an artificial construct, Med somehow sounded contrite. *"I apologize Robert. I did not mean to intrude. I will stop speaking now."*

Robert turned toward Sarah as each stared deeply into the other's eyes.

She met his gaze without wavering.

As their lips began to move closer, a passing bicyclist yelled out, "Kiss her already!"

They both turned toward the cyclist, smiled, and completed the kiss.

When their lips parted, Sarah glanced away from Robert, trying to hide the blush on her face. "I'll admit, I've been wanting to do that for a while."

"Me too," Robert said with a foolish grin.

"I'm so happy we came here."

From behind them, a gruff voice snarled, "I'm happy yah did, too. Now hand over your wallet bub, and I'll take your purse too, dollie."

Both whirled to look behind them and were shocked to see a rough looking man pointing a gun at them. Robert's first thought was for Sarah's safety.

Med, can you cloak a tendril into his gun barrel?

"*I thought you wanted me to be quiet?*" asked Med, instead of immediately complying with the request.

Circumstances have changed. Wait till I stand up and— Hold it! I have a better idea. Can you produce a blue light man standing behind him and have it tell him to put the gun down?

"*That is quite imaginative, but it will not accomplish much, being only an empty energy shell.*"

Just do it!

"*Very well.*"

Behind the robber suddenly appeared Blue Light, whose mechanical sounding voice boomed, "Put that gun down."

The gunman looked behind him and quickly changed his tune. "Blue Light! Don't hoit me. I'll put down the gat," but instead quickly shot at the blue glowing man.

Like a fool he emptied his gun into him. Yet the bullets went right through the glow and whined off into the distance before they hit something solid!

With the thief's back to them and his gun emptied, Robert yanked him by the collar backwards over the bench. He grabbed the now useless weapon from his hand and used it to clobber the would-be robber upside the head.

The crook groaned and lost consciousness. With that Robert let go and allowed him to fall to the ground as Med's phantom Blue Light disappeared. Ackers never noticed. He was more concerned about Sarah. "Are you all right? He didn't hurt you?"

"I'm okay. He never touched me." She was shaking though and he took

"Now hand over your wallet, bub."

her in his arms. "Was that thing behind him the Blue Light?"

"It must've been. I have no idea where he came from but I sure am glad he showed up." *No talking right now Med. Just keep this guy tied down for me,* he warned mentally, sensing that the medallion was about to protest his deception. "Did you see where he went?" he asked Sarah in what he hoped sounded like an earnest voice. "I wanted to thank him."

"No I didn't, but I'm glad he was here too. You didn't get hurt?" Sarah asked in a fearful voice.

"No I'm fine," he answered, "but I'm sorry this had to spoil our day together."

"Why are you sorry?" Sarah insisted. "With Blue Light's aid you protected me. If I had been alone, I don't know what would have happened!" She began to break down and he held her closer.

"I know Sarah," he said into her hair as she sobbed on his shoulder, "and that is what concerns me the most. Crime is definitely getting worse in this area. I was worried that with the argument we had earlier and all, that well— Maybe you'd change you mind about me and I wouldn't be able to see you anymore."

Sarah looked up, her eyes red-rimmed, and she placed her hand on his arm. "No Robert. This was an... an awful experience. But it wasn't your fault. And you did the right thing, with Blue Light's help. I can see now that these bad people just kind of appear wherever you are."

That was a sobering thought for Ackers. These criminals did seem to be showing up rather regularly wherever he seemed to be, didn't they? Was that because of Med, or was he somehow a target for them?

The would-be robber began to groan and stir, and Ackers looked down at him in consternation. Sarah was trembling. "I wonder if there's an officer nearby?" she said in a tremulous tone.

Robert knew somebody should be on the way. Those shots had been loud. Their area of the park had cleared out. *Med, are any of the police force on the way yet?*

"Yes Robert, there is an officer just entering the park."

Good!

"I see one beyond the fence over there," Robert said before calling out, "Officer! We need you over here!"

Considering it was his beat, Hadley came running toward the call for help, sidearm in hand. "There was a report of shots fired so there should be a squad car on the way as we speak. Are you folks injured?" Then he stopped in his tracks and holstered his weapon. "Oh, it's you Mister Ackers.

And this is Miss Sarah, am I right?" He already had his cuffs out for the third party who was just barely coming around.

Let go of the criminal Med. Officer Hadley will handle him now.

"Yes, that's me," Sarah replied, wiping her face before pointing down at the limp man at their feet, the gun a few feet away. "That man was going to rob us. At least he would have, but the Blue Light showed up, and when the man turned toward him and began to shoot, Robert pulled him down and hit him with his own gun."

"Hit him pretty hard, too, from what I can see," observed Hadley as he rolled the groaning man over and cuffed him. "So, Blue Light was here? Did you see where he went?" Hadley stood up and with a notepad and pencil pulled from a pocket; he began to scribble down what they had told him.

"No. He just disappeared as suddenly as he appeared," replied Robert.

"Yeah, he seems to do that an awful lot," Hadley said with a frown as he picked up the gun and placed it in his belt.

It was then that the crook finally regained consciousness. "What hit me? A hammer?"

"Get up yah bum," ordered Hadley, dragging him to his feet.

As he started to shove the prisoner along, Hadley called back to Robert, "You know the drill, so I assume you'll come by later and fill out the witness forms, right?"

Sarah answered for him. "Yes officer. We both will. Thank you."

"Just doing my job Miss," he said, and then gave her a smile. "Thanks is more due to your boyfriend because he's the one who actually took the big risks."

As cop and criminal walked away, Robert faced Sarah and smiled. "Well, maybe we can go back to doing what we were doing?"

"Not here!" she said, for that part of the day for her had been ruined. "How about we go to the movies instead," Sarah asked in return. She looked at her watch. "We could still catch the matinee if we hurry. You said Clark Gable was playing?"

"Yes. Maybe we can still get seats in the back. Where it's dark."

"Yeah, because I look a wreck right now and I don't want to sit near anyone but you!" Sarah said with vehemence. With that they left the park quietly with his arm around her, though Ackers kept a far closer eye on what was happening nearby.

+++

"Robert, was the Blue Light construct satisfactory?" Med asked.

It did the job, thank you. Do you know where the bullets went? He'd been afraid that others might have been injured.

"Do not be concerned. I directed them into a tree. It scared one of those four footed animals Sarah called a squirrel. The creature is physically unhurt but it was quite frightened. It scrambled up the other side of the tree and said some very unpleasant things."

It was a bit of a surprise that Med could understand squirrel chatter, but Ackers filed that knowledge away for now. *Good. Please keep an eye out for other trouble, but if none comes, don't interrupt us, okay?*

"Got it boss."

That's cute, but frankly I think of us as partners, although one of us is a VERY silent partner.

"Very subtle Robert. Is it still acceptable to you if I observe your mating dance with Sarah?"

There was the mental version of a frustrated sigh. *Can I stop you?*

"To be honest, no."

Didn't think so. We'll speak about it later. MUCH later.

Sarah, not realizing the other conversation he was having, observed, "You're very quiet."

"Just enjoying the company and the walk," Robert said with a reassuring smile.

+++

The movie did help settle things down. Because it was a pleasant afternoon, the theater was not crowded. Most of the patrons seemed to prefer the seats up toward the front and middle, so they had a section in the back all to themselves. With popcorn from a street vendor outside smuggled in under Robert's jacket, they sat munching in silence until the ten cent bag was gone. There were newsreels and a cartoon, along with the feature film. During the love scenes there were a few smooches and sighs, and Robert Ackers was the happiest man on earth. The matinee was the best fifty cents he'd ever spent!

When they left the theater, he remembered that his landlady had wanted to have them over to dinner. "Sarah," he said, "I would gladly take you out to eat, but I think Mrs. Mondella would feel hurt if we didn't come by and have dinner with her. Would you be okay with that?"

She looked up at him. "After the day we had? I'd much rather sit with her and you than in some crowded restaurant." She looked down at her clothes and sighed. "That is, if you think I'm dressed properly."

Robert chuckled. Women were awfully vain about their appearance. "I think you look fine. She's a widow Sarah, and other than her renters, she doesn't get much company. I think she'd be thrilled to have you to dinner. She does make a fantastic spaghetti and meatballs. Of course she's going to ask a lot of questions."

"I'll answer the ones I can," Sarah said sweetly, so her mind was made up. They would be guests of Mrs. Mondella for the evening, and that would make his landlady very happy indeed.

+++

Later that night, bellies stuffed with dinner and dessert, they said a long goodbye out on the apartment building stoop. Mrs. Mondella had refused to let them help with the dishes.

"You two lover birds go now, I got dis," she insisted. "And you come back again to see me Sarah, I like you very much."

Sarah had been sent home in a cab, and his landlady stuck her head out her door as a very happy Robert Ackers came back inside and locked the entranceway after him.

"That one you should marry young man," she said firmly from her doorway. "Don't let her get away."

"I won't," he promised with a big, dumb grin.

He returned to his apartment and prepared for bed, in a very good mood as Med observed, *"I assume I may talk to you now? At Ackers affirmation, Med went on, "This afternoon at the theater was an interesting experience. Yet why did you sit so far in the back? There were seats much closer. And neither you nor Sarah seemed to be watching what was projected on the screen. I found the presentation interesting. Was that a true story?"*

Robert smiled at the memory, and mentally replied, *No. It was a fictional piece.*

"Well, it was quite enlightening about human interaction between the genders. But this was purely for entertainment purposes?"

Yes. Some things, like news reports and documentaries aren't fictional. I think a couple played before the movie.

"I noticed your attention was not on the projection."

Robert grinned more broadly. *You better believe it!*

Med paused before asking, *"Was that another step in the mating ritual?"*

Ackers paused before responding, *I guess you could call it that.*

"Then what is the next step?"

Robert contemplated what to say before telling Med, *That depends on how fast Sarah wants to go.*

"The woman sets the ritual's pace?"

Like most things, it's a mutual... ah— understanding. If we move too fast it could ruin the relationship. The same if we move too slowly. So we kinda feel out each step as we go along.

"How do you know when to go to the next steps? What are they?"

Ackers sighed in resignation. He didn't really mind having someone to talk to about his burgeoning relationship with Sarah, and he had known these questions would be forthcoming. Still, it wasn't always easy to explain to Med, who had no human emotions.

Well, there are several components to a human courtship. Physical, emotional, mental. We need to see if we have similar goals, interests and the like. That requires a lot of talking. Learning to trust each other and be truthful with our responses.

"Which, unfortunately you cannot reciprocate in regards to anything concerning Blue Light," Med interjected.

Ackers sighed in frustration this time. *Please, don't remind me. I feel bad enough lying to Sarah as it is. I'd rather just focus on the positive parts of today.*

"Noted. What of the more physical aspects of this mating ritual?"

I don't like how you keep bringing that up! Robert said, feeling uneasy. *We also move in steps there. Most couples move slowly. First we kiss. Then, at some point, things get more— intimate. This isn't something that can be planned.*

"How long does this take?"

It varies. Different speeds for different people. In my culture, we can take months or years. Some go at breakneck speed and race through everything in hours. Days at most.

"Are the shorter relationships viable?"

Some, but not all. Most people eventually get married, where you agree to legally remain involved with only one person for life. Some relationships unfortunately end in separation or divorce.

"What is this divorce?"

People who don't have a successful marriage separate and go on with their lives, hoping their next attempt at a relationship will be successful. Yet not all separations go well. Either party can initiate the proceedings, which sometimes surprises the other party. *Those can become messy and emotional. If they get married, and find out they weren't compatible after all and want to be separate again, they get a divorce. It's a legal separation that ends a marriage. How things they own are split up and where any children involved will live is not always mutually agreed upon after finding out how the other person feels. So divorce can be complicated and must be handled through a court.*

"So if they are not married, they separate. If they are, they get a divorce?"

Basically, yes.

"I heard your landlady mention marriage as you came back indoors for the evening. What is this marriage like?"

Med, you ask so many complex questions! Another sigh. *After a period, if the couple both want to, they go through a ritual called a wedding, where generally a religious figure or at least someone the law says is capable presides over the ceremony. It varies according to one or both of their faiths what happens during the wedding. It can also be done in a secular way if preferred.*

"Will you and Sarah go through this process?"

Now Med was getting into territory that Robert wasn't quite ready to contemplate. It had been a long and eventful day and he'd rather concentrate on something else.

I think that's enough questions for tonight Med. Despite the hour, my stomach is too full and I'm not sleepy yet, so I'm going to try to write for a while.

"Very well. I will keep watch."

You do that.

CHAPTER 18

Captain Rogen was working late in his office when Officer Hadley, dressed in civilian clothes since he was off duty for the night, entered.

"Here are those reports you wanted to see, sir," Hadley said, setting them on the Captain's desk.

"Ah yes. That collar you made today, the armed robbery," Rogen began, while scanning the forms. "Interesting— So Robert Ackers was there with his girlfriend Sarah?"

"Yes, sir," answered Hadley. "They were the crook's intended targets.

Attempted purse and wallet snatching."

"I see. And Blue Light was also there?"

"So they said. The gunman said it too. Claims he shot him. It. Whatever."

"He shot Blue Light?" Rogen asked in disbelief.

"Yes, sir. Emptied his weapon into him is what Ackers claimed, and that was when he yanked the goon back and pistol whipped him with his own weapon."

"Impressive." It actually was, especially for that mousy little guy. "I also see that Blue Light got away again. Did you find the slugs on the ground?"

"No, sir, just some spent brass. The guy said the bullets went straight through him."

Rogen was surprised to hear this. "Bullets went through Blue Light?"

"Yes, sir. Through. And his description of Blue Light was different from others we've gotten."

This was new. Rogen sat up and set the pages down rather than reading more. "Different how?"

"Past reports say inside Blue Light was a man shape. This time the description doesn't include that. Or at least, the guy I collared didn't report it."

"What do you mean?"

"The crook says it was nothing but a solid bright blue man shaped light and his bullets went straight through because there was nothing inside. Yet the other witnesses don't agree."

"How?"

"Ackers says there was a shape within the light, but the crook was nervous facing Blue Light to begin with and his shots went wild. The lady told me she didn't have a good angle to tell what, if anything, might have been inside the light and that it all happened too fast to say anything other than the crook did shoot at the light."

"Thank you Hadley. You may go. Enjoy your downtime."

"Thank you sir." Hadley left.

Alone, Rogen wondered what the differences could mean. *What is this Blue Light? A man surrounded by light or something else? How does it work?*

Yet there were even more important questions on the Captain's mind.

How are you tied into all of this Robert Ackers? Are you the Blue Light or do you just have some connection to it so you're always protected? Either way, what do I do with the information once I know for sure? Who can I trust to tell?

+++

On the far side of downtown, a well dressed representative of the new Uptown Boss sat in Ricco's office, directing what was left of Ricco's men in how things should be done from now on. He was introduced to the remainder of the gang by Sammy as simply 'Mr. Beta' and offered no further information about himself than that. When the door opened he looked up with a frown on his narrow face with its light shadow of beard and thin mustache. His ice blue eyes were always analytically cold, but nonetheless he was pleased to see Spats come into the office and announced, "I got all the stuff you told me we'd need."

"The explosives as well?" Beta asked with an edge to his voice. These people needed to learn to knock and show some respect.

Spats caught on quickly and he toned it down.

"Everything Boss, though I had to make a case for them before those guys would sell to me. They were awful suspicious until I told them you had ordered them." He grinned and the man sitting at the desk simply nodded. "So why did we need so many different kinds of explosives?"

Beta gave him a smug smile that barely lifted his thin upper lip and mustache, and said, "For your information, we need them all because we don't know which kind will be the most effective against Blue Light. Maybe only one type, maybe all of them. Either way we want to be certain. What about the location?"

"Got that too," Spats said proudly. "It's a large new construction on the East side. Only one guard at night."

The man finally smiled and nodded his approval. "Sounds perfect. The crews aren't working on it at night, are they?"

"No. They just broke ground two weeks ago and are a long ways off from deadline.

"Fine then." He drummed his fingers, several of which bore expensive rings with diamonds and gold, and then pointed a long forefinger at Spats. "Now I want you to collect everyone with explosives experience that your people have. We want this set up two nights from now. That will make it Friday night, so there will be no interference over the weekend. Then we'll need to spread the rumor about something going on there—maybe a street gang dust up—including the where and the when. Our employer needs it ready to go by Saturday night. Sunday night at the absolute latest, because there will be enough moon to see by. We don't want that bright blue fellow sneaking up on us in the darkness because he seems to be able to turn his light on and off at will. Got that?"

"Okay. Then what?" Spats asked.

"Your people will go in and set up the trap after the construction closes for the day; that should be around five. Wait until everyone clears out. Get someone to find us a drawing of the lot. We'll use that to choose the best places to put the explosives, but I want to be able to set them off remotely so none of our boys get hurt. Can we do that?"

Spats smiled. "Yeah sure. Might take a little longer. Wiring should probably wait until Saturday morning though so we can see what we're doing. What about the guard? If we off him someone will find out and we're screwed."

Beta shook his head. "We will handle the guard and he won't bother you. Okay, now get going. I want that drawing by tomorrow afternoon," he ordered.

Spats left and once he was gone, shutting the door behind him, Beta made a phone call. When someone picked up he said, "Somebody better locate and send me Little Ned. Tell him I want to see him right away today, while I'm in the area, so he better not dawdle." He hung up, not waiting for the answer and sat back in the chair to contemplate what came next until Ned got there.

Ned was a useful kid, a gang wannabe, but smarter than the average mug. He was someone their employer wanted groomed for a position above this cheap street thug level. Ned was a sneaky little bastard who could get around and into places without being noticed, but he sometimes took too long to bring back viable information. They'd had him following someone and he had yet to report. It was high time he did.

Their employer wanted this Blue Light character to be history and was willing to spare no expense to do that. The glowing crusader showing up so frequently was throwing a big monkey wrench into any funding they could raise to take over this end of the city and eventually the entire area. There were other contenders for that sort of position too and so they'd either have to be bought off or eliminated. All that would cost quite a bit of cash. So the munitions thing had been cooked up to see if they could permanently end this do-gooder's current hero status and show the public who the real muscle was. If that didn't work, they'd have to get to Blue Light some other way. Whatever that thing was it had to go—and soon.

This Blue Light seemed to have a friend or some connection in this Robert Ackers guy, who also had come out of nowhere. Ackers was now a person of interest. Their connection in the police department agreed with that. Ackers kept showing up on reports that had anything to do with Blue Light appearances. So if they could not get Blue Light in the explosion, they'd definitely get Ackers instead and then let his capture lure the crime fighter in. By now Little Ned, who had been keeping an eye on Ackers, should have some idea of what they needed to do to reel the guy in.

It had been noted that Ackers also had a girlfriend, some young babe who worked at that downtown diner whose owner refused to pay for protection. They'd deal with the stubborn owner later on. Right now Ned was supposed to set something up to get her full name and address. They couldn't take her at work but if she lived alone, she was fair game.

Ned had been told not to share this information with the locals, who were all small time gangs hiring street thugs. So far they'd only been useful in racketeering, their shakedowns and reprisals for noncompliance had been far too loud and obvious. They depended excessively on petty crimes and extortion to bring in money, and their attempts at setting up for selling drugs or pulling bank jobs had been sloppy at best. This was why the uptown folks insisted that their own people would handle the next part of the plan, because it must be done quietly and efficiently. No more blunders or they would all be replaced.

Once they had accumulated enough money to buy off whomever couldn't simply be eliminated, then they would fully take over. That's when things would always be done the new boss' way.

It had been an uphill climb, but this end of the city was going to be under their control within a few months. Already the police were at a crossroads where either they'd have to look the other way or declare war on the gangs, only to find themselves outclassed and outnumbered. So far the Feds had not been notified and with the right words whispered in the proper ears, that was not going to happen. The official position was that this was all small time crime and the local precinct should be able to handle it without federal backup. That attitude of indifference had cost very little in actual bribes because someone who couldn't afford to have his personal vices made public had been leaned on to call in some favors. It helped to have acquaintances in high places with low morals.

+++

From what Ned had caught of the lovebirds' parting conversation, Ackers had refused to let his girlfriend walk home and insisted she take a cab at his expense. Guy either had deep pockets or he was really gone on this gal. She was a cutie!

When the cab pulled up to the apartment building where Ackers lived and the babe got in, Ackers paid the driver with pocket change. Ned took note of the company and the number before it left in case he lost track of it along the route. There was no way he could follow on foot without running and that would make him stand out in the crowd. He knew he'd eventually lose it in traffic when they got to the bigger avenues. So he kept an eye on it as long as possible and noted the general direction it was headed. While he kept pace well behind, he did some thinking.

Ricco had never thought of tailing Ackers and finding out about his girlfriend. Ned had, and his information was why Beta had brought him in. Ned figured if she regularly walked to work, she couldn't live very far away from the diner. That kind of job didn't pay too well, so she'd still be in the lower rent district. She had walked over to Ackers' apartment building as well, so wherever she lived wasn't far from his place either. She didn't look like the tenement type, so then it must be one of the old houses that had been turned into apartments that got rented out, something like where Ackers lived.

That had all checked out.

Not many people in their area could afford cabs, so until they got to the more congested areas, Ned was able to keep it in sight. When traffic finally began picking up and the cabbie had to slow down some to remain in the proper lane, Ned didn't want to be seen. He took a chance and cut through a couple alleys to get ahead of the cab. He spotted it once he came back out on the sidewalk, making a turn onto a side street just up ahead where he knew there was an apartment building in a quiet section. It was a little better quality place than he had expected, and farther from the diner too, so maybe that's why she was reluctant to take the cab even after being assaulted that day. She was tapped out with rent.

He had to race through some back lots to get there, but made it just in time to see her go up to one of the doors and let herself inside. Then Ned headed back toward where the diner was, to see if that was still open and he could get some personal information about her.

At least he knew her first name from hearing them argue about the cab. Ned had an alibi for stopping by her workplace tucked into his shirt. Something that he had pinched from another woman who was unloading her groceries from the boot of the family car and had left it too conveniently within reach.

It took him a while to get back to the diner, which at that hour was closing, the dinner crowd having petered out. He came in anyway and the cashier looked up and shook her head.

"I'm sorry sir, but we can't serve you now. We're closed for the day," she said with an apologetic smile.

"Oh that's okay ma'am," Ned said politely, doffing his hat and giving her a big friendly grin. His boyish charisma and open countenance always charmed the ladies. "I just came in looking for a Sarah who works here. You see, she took a Yellow Cab today and left something in there that the company asked me to return to her. Is she still here?"

"Oh dear," the woman said. "Today was her day off. I can take it and lock it in the safe."

"Uh, no ma'am," he said and shook his head. "My boss told me to give it to Sarah and Sarah only." He pulled a small purse out of his shirt and flashed it briefly. "Do you know where she lives and what her last name is? I need to get this to her right away, before she calls the police and tells them one of our drivers made off with it. Even if it's all a mistake, that's bad publicity for the company you know," he added in a conspiratorial whisper. "Plus I'm kind of nervous holding it for her. There might be money and other stuff inside that she needs. I didn't look. Honest I didn't," he added with a sheepish shrug.

"Aren't you a fine young man!" the older woman said with a big smile. Pulling an order slip off the counter she turned it over and wrote down Sarah's full name and address and handed it to him. "Here you go. Please come back and have a meal on the house here sometime. The owner is my cousin and we all adore Sarah. Our food is top notch," she added.

"I'll surely do that ma'am," he said with that same friendly grin while tucking the paper into his pocket after scanning it. Then he tipped his cap before shoving it back on his head and turned to leave the diner.

Sarah Baker would not be getting a visitor tonight, because Ned still had to head down to the warehouse district to drop that information off. At least when they did send someone after her, they would know the right time and place to intercept her. They'd likely snatch her somewhere on her way home. Having the address written down would be a big help, Ned figured he might get a bonus for that. If not, at least he'd get to keep all that was in the purse. Nobody else knew about it, though it sure had come in handy.

Shame though. That Sarah was a nice looking doll. Still, a fellow had to make his money where he could. Ned hoped they wouldn't rough her up too much.

+++

With Ned's report and the address of Ackers' waitress girlfriend known, a secondary plan was put into place. First though the explosives had to be set up and that would take some finesse. The Uptown Boss insisted they put a demolitions expert in charge, so someone had been hired to oversee the placement of the explosives and the local gang guys were used as laborers. It was going to make a mess of the site, but that was someone else's problem. As long as it took out Blue Light, it would be worth the money spent behind the scenes to keep the bigger plans feasible.

The guy they brought in was good. He'd been involved in mining down in Harlan County, Kentucky, and got himself blacklisted for union organizing. Because he couldn't work in the mines anymore and his family had to be fed, he took demolitions jobs wherever he could find them, asking no questions as long as he got paid. The Uptown Boss had heard of him somewhere and so he was brought in because he was affordable with a good reputation. All he had to do to get paid and move on was tell them where the stuff should be placed and make sure it was set up properly. The site had been passed off as an abandoned construction when the builder went belly-up that would become a new site for someone who bought it for pennies on the dollar. Everyone involved had been told to repeat that story, and this guy wasn't going to ask unnecessary questions anyway.

The equipment was dropped off Friday night, after the site guard was prevented from being any kind of witness. They wouldn't find him for a long, long time and by then it would appear to be an accident. In case a patrol car came by, another man about the guard's height and build was now wearing his clothing and helmet while carrying the flashlight. The replacement took his usual stand outside the gate and walked his regular rounds.

Most of the stuff could be put in place that night, so only the fine wiring and connections to detonators had to wait for first light. When all was in readiness, the crew erased any obvious trace of their presence and left. With the gate securely locked again, they weren't too worried about the day guard. Reports said he never went inside. Someone would keep watch though and if he got nosy, he'd join his nighttime buddy under concrete. There was always some place nearby with wet cement.

+++

The movie and cab fare had set Ackers back a bit. Money was tight these days and jobs scarce, but Robert made somewhat of a comfortable income with the stories he sold, as long as he was careful about expenses. Living right in the city, the postage for mailing in manuscripts wasn't too steep. He was a relatively fast and prolific writer with a good imagination so had little problem selling his stuff, though as a steady source of income, it definitely depended on getting things written and out to the magazines as quickly as possible. There were plenty of other hungry writers they could turn to for filler material.

Lately, since finding the medallion, Robert had not written often enough. And tonight, as much as he wanted to write, his mind kept wandering over the day's events. The walk to the park and sitting there with Sarah had been like a dream come true, until the attempted purse snatching. The fight with the robber with Med trying to emulate Blue Light without surrounding him had worked, though it seemed to have wearied both of them. The movie had been almost an afterthought for Ackers, who had been struggling to calm down and think rationally, though having his arm around Sarah, kissing her, and feeling her relax in his presence had been worth sitting woodenly through it. He could still recall the smell of her hair when her head was on his shoulder.

The dinner with Mrs. Mondella had actually gone quite well too, even with his landlady's gentle but somewhat obvious suggestions about courtship and marriage. Sarah blushed a lot, but otherwise she didn't seem to mind. She found Mrs. Mondella charming and had listened with a sympathetic ear to tales of her late husband's adventures and virtues.

Sarah was kind and caring that way. She was almost exactly the sort of girl that Robert had been looking for. She was a prize and he wanted to do right by her. But then there was Med and the incredible powers it granted Robert and all the things they could accomplish together that would help other people live better, safer lives—especially with the rising crime in their area. Of course there was also his writing, which was not just an income source, but something he enjoyed doing. Could he support both Sarah and himself with his writing and still continue his fight against the lawlessness that was so pervasive in his area? How could he possibly make it all work?

It was twenty minutes past midnight when Robert finally sat back in his chair and sighed in resignation. Only half a page written, and that hard fought for. He took off his glasses and set them down on the desk, scrubbing his tired eyes with the palms of his hands before running fingers up into his hair. He should just get some sleep; he wasn't going to get any more done tonight. He had to go down to the police station sometime tomorrow—today, he realized, looking at the clock. Grabbing his glasses, he shut off the desk lamp and staggered tiredly over to the bed to flop down after placing both his specs and Med on the nightstand. The alarm wound and set for eight a.m., Robert Ackers was almost instantly asleep.

But even in 1931, New York City never slept. There was always something happening somewhere—

+++

"There's been a change in plans," Beta told Sammy and Spats when they came to tell him Saturday morning that the setup was done and the man from Kentucky had been paid. "The Alpha," which was what he had been calling the Uptown Boss the last several days, "wants the girl taken immediately and brought to the site. We don't want her down in the yard. We just want it known she's out there somewhere."

"Won't that draw Ackers to the site?" Sammy, who was quickest to pick up on such things, asked.

Beta smiled thinly. "That's exactly the idea. Our eyes and ears in the local precinct tell us that their captain has also caught on that Ackers and Blue Light keep showing up together. So there must be some connection. Bring in the girl and you're bound to have them both there at the same time. We get Blue Light with the explosives. Ackers buys it the old fashioned way and we let the world think they took each other out."

Sammy lifted an eyebrow, but Spats was enthusiastic. "Hey, that might work! Kill two birds with one stone like they say."

"As long as Ackers doesn't call the police first," Sammy said thoughtfully.

"If he does, it will be handled," Beta answered but didn't elaborate and Sammy knew better than to ask how. While he and Sammy didn't get along well because they were essentially vying for the same position, Beta did appreciate the man's intelligence and ability to think ahead and not overreact. This Sammy was one cool-headed character, and if he played his cards right, he might get the local level boss' job.

If not, he'd get his name in the papers, the hard way.

"How do we get the message to Ackers that his little chippie is in danger?" Spats asked.

Sammy winced as Beta frowned at Spats, because as much as the Baker girl was expendable, he didn't like her being referred to as a whore. Spats looked down, not knowing what he said but realizing he'd better clam up now and listen.

"We let *Miss Sarah*," he stressed her name so the halfwit lummox would maybe catch on, "call him from somewhere. Hearing her scared voice sobbing into the phone ought to shake him up some and bring him directly to us on the run."

"One little problem with that," Sammy said quietly. "Ackers has no phone. There's one in his building that they all use, but there's no telling who might answer and whether the message will get relayed. Might be better to send him a note with something of hers so that he won't mistake it for a ruse."

"Good idea," Beta said after a pause, and he gave Sammy a frank and calculating look that was not mistaken. This was a man worth keeping.

"So get things moving," Beta said in a tone of dismissal. "This goes down tonight."

CHAPTER 19

Frank & Di's Diner opened as early as 6 a.m. on weekdays and closed after seven most evenings when the working crowd left the area. It was usually busy and the same waitresses staffed the place all day. The hours were lengthy but Frank couldn't afford to hire any more help. He ran the grills out back, Diana the cash register and occasionally the counter and since they were both in by 4 a.m. to prep food, their days were longer than anyone else's. Sarah and the other waitress Mildred only had to be in fifteen minutes before opening time. It was a long day on their feet, though like most people who still had jobs they worked without complaint, just glad to not be eating in soup kitchens or standing in bread lines and sleeping in a flophouse.

Sarah had been working a lot lately, so she was glad to have gotten a day off, even if it was a Friday. Saturdays were busy too and since Mildred needed this one off to attend a wedding, Sarah had to both wait on and bus the entire diner by herself. She was plenty tired by closing time, but at least on Saturdays that was by noon. Now she could go home, relax, soak her feet and know that she had tomorrow off as well. Frank didn't open on Sundays.

The last lingering customer finished his coffee and pie and left without leaving a tip as Diana shut and locked the door behind him. "Cheapskate!" she snapped under her breath. He could have at least left a few pennies

"So get this moving," Beta said. "This goes down tonight."

for poor Sarah who, in spite of her outwardly cheerful manner, had run her legs off all morning. Now that the door was locked and the open sign turned around to say 'CLOSED', Diana cashed out her drawer and turned the interior lights off.

While Sarah was getting her jacket and purse, the cashier walked out back to lock the money in the safe, which gave her a chance to speak to the girl. "I'm sorry Honey, but that last guy stiffed you. For all the time he was here sucking down java, he could have at least left you a small tip."

Sarah shrugged. "I noticed, but that's the way it goes these days. Hard times for a lot of folks."

Diana wasn't satisfied. "Well I'm not buying that. For one thing, he could afford coffee and pie, and also he bought a newspaper, because he had it up in front of his face the whole time, reading it from one end to the other. That tells me he wasn't flat broke, just antisocial and stingy.

"But anyway I never got a chance to ask you, how was your day off?" the older woman added, all smiles now. She had noted that Ackers fellow had not been in yesterday, nor had he shown up this morning. Also interesting was that Sarah had been quiet and thoughtful most of the day. She hoped they hadn't broken up already!

"Well— it was lot more exciting than I wanted or expected, though most of it was very nice," Sarah admitted.

Glad of the chance to talk to someone, she told her coworker about the walk in the park with Robert and then the attempted robbery, and how Ackers had fought the man off. Diana seemed properly shocked but was also intrigued and urged her to elaborate. "Just as things were getting intense that Blue Light guy showed up and that scared the robber so much that he actually shot at it!"

Sarah gave a shiver that was no act. Diana gasped in disbelief and her eyes went wide. "The bullets didn't even hurt Blue Light. They just went right through him; or at least that's what I was told. I didn't see that part because I was so panicked, I just ducked and prayed for it to be over. Once the robber was out of bullets, somehow Robert managed to knock the guy out. A police officer showed up right after that, though by then Blue Light was gone. At that point I was a wreck," she admitted and Diana gave her a big sympathetic hug as they walked out front again together.

"Oh how awful all that must have been for you! But your Robert is a special young man. Sarah, you must be so proud of him," Diana said in a dreamy tone.

"Yeah I am, but I really don't like him being involved in this stuff. He could get seriously hurt—or worse!"

"I know, but he is very brave and capable from what I've seen." Diana shuddered a little bit too, recalling the attempted robbery and shakedown of the diner that Ackers had helped foil. She and Frank really owed him a lot for that, the diner was their only source of income. After his hitch in the service where he had learned to cook, her cousin Frank had pooled all his meager resources into buying the place and fixing it up. The diner was his life's work and it was keeping both of them afloat in these hard times. Frank was a tough little guy who wasn't about to let some two-bit gangland mugs bleed him dry. They were just scraping by every month as it was.

"Don't get me wrong, I am happy with Robert for the most part," Sarah admitted, "but I'm also worried about him. I don't want him getting into all these fights and playing the hero. He's a nice guy and I admire his courage, but this stuff frightens me. Let that Blue Light character and the police handle things and let's just live quietly."

"I know, it concerns us too. Frank talks to a lot of the local business owners and they've all been getting pressure to pay for 'insurance' so that their place doesn't get busted up. It just the times we live in—" Diana let the subject drop there. "But you did have a nice day, other that that one incident in the park?" She wanted to hear the pleasant parts.

Sarah nodded as she put on her jacket and shouldered her plain tan purse. "Oh sure! We went to a matinee and saw a Clark Gable movie. Something recent, but you'll have to forgive me because I was still rattled at the time so I've forgotten the title. It was a long day. Plus the movie had gangster stuff in it too, so at that point I kind of tuned it out. I don't know why such a handsome and talented actor keeps taking these roles as gangsters though. Don't we have enough of that in real life?"

Sarah seemed rather stuck on the topic so Diana said some soothing words as they walked out the side door together and she locked it behind them. She was waiting for a ride home from her cousin, who had to get his car out of the back lot, which was tricky and narrow. "At least you both got to relax a bit, right?" she asked, still fishing for more intimate information.

"Yeah, we did," Sarah said with a half smile, remembering the cozier moments. "After the movie we walked back to his place and had dinner with his landlady. She's very nice and a fabulous cook. Mrs. Mondella is Italian, so she makes excellent spaghetti and meatballs. As good as the restaurants. She's a widow and very lonely, and really talkative. She did kind of prod Robert and me a lot about our future plans." Diana's eyes lit up and Sarah could tell she was about to broaden that discussion. "We're nowhere near that stage yet," she added to forestall further nosy questions. Thankfully Frank was finally coming up with the car!

"Hey Doll, you want a ride home too?" he asked with a grin. Frank was always a tease.

"No. It's nice out today, so I'll walk," Sarah said with an answering smile, coming over to his side where the window was open to the afternoon breeze. Diana opened the passenger side door to get in. Tossing her purse in the back seat, she tucked in her skirt and made to slide over, and then stopped with the door still open and slapped her forehead.

"Where is my brain today! We were so busy this morning and then we got to talking, I forgot to tell you something that happened yesterday. A nice young man from the cab company stopped by at closing time to return your purse. He said you left it in the cab and the company insisted he take it straight out to you. You did get it, right?" she added, looking at the usual simple tan bag that Sarah always brought to work. The one the youth showed her was far fancier, with needlepoint flowers and a gold colored chain and clasp.

Sarah gave her a strange look. "No! I did take a cab home because Robert insisted and he paid for it, but I had my purse with me the whole time." She patted the one on her shoulder, clamped under her arm. "I have no idea why they thought it was mine. Someone else must have left it in there. I don't even recall seeing it."

"Well he said the driver told them it was yours," Diana remembered, "I didn't think it looked like anything you've ever used. In fact it was pretty expensive bag, come to think of it."

"That's sort of odd, but I suppose mistakes get made now and then," Sarah said in a subdued tone. The idea of it being a purse and a strange man coming to ask for her by name made her somewhat uneasy after yesterday's incident in the park.

"C'mon ladies. Time and gas is wasting here while you're flapping your gums," Frank urged. He was dying for that first beer of the day. One of the better perks of being a New Yorker was that Prohibition measures had been repealed back in 1923, and rightfully so, Frank had always insisted.

"You're probably right. It was just a mistake," Diana admitted and she got in and slammed the door. But she leaned past Frank to continue through his open window. "Sarah, he asked for your address so he could return it and I gave it to him. I hope that's okay."

"Should be fine. He never came by anyway," Sarah said with a reassuring nod. Something about the situation didn't feel right, but she figured she was still jumpy after yesterday's incident and let it go at that. Recent events had left her a bit unnerved, but not enough to accept a ride from Frank, who at almost twice her age, balding, and unmarried was still a bit of a flirt. Plus he always smelled of sweat mingled with the smoke and grease of the grill that he tended all day. He'd drop Diana off first and then he'd drive really slow with his arm on the back of her seat, and Sarah would have to make small talk with him all the way to her place. "I'll see you Monday," she added, and watched them drive away with a bit of relief.

Then Sarah started on her way home as well, trudging along anxiously, a lot less thrilled with the beautiful afternoon weather than she had been when her shift ended.

+++

They had chosen the spot well. It was on a quiet side street near a used car lot that was closed for the day. So the big black sedan parked among the other vehicles did not stand out as she walked by.

When the man who had been ambling along well behind her for some time quickened his pace, Sarah Baker turned for a moment, and that's when she realized it was the tightwad from the diner. He never slowed down but just kept coming. Clutching her purse close to her body, she turned and walked faster. He picked up the pace so she panicked and began to run. He ran too.

The block heel on one of her Oxford pumps caught in a crack on the buckled sidewalk and Sarah fell, skinning a knee and ripping her stockings. Scrambling to her feet, she limped off again, but was so intent on outdistancing the man behind her; she did not see the burly guy who came out from between the two nearest cars in the lot, with a saturated piece of surgical sponge folded into a handkerchief. He grabbed her in an iron grip and clapped his big hand over her nose and mouth.

Sarah struggled and tried to scream but couldn't. Kicking, scratching, biting, she thrashed about as he hung on grimly with arms like a gorilla wrapped around her until that sickly sweet vapor left her unconscious. Then trailed by his accomplice, he lifted her up and carried her slight, limp form back between the parked cars before anyone else might pass by.

She was out cold when they hauled her like a sack of grain into their waiting car. They trussed her up and gagged her. Then the big man shoved her face down in the back on the floor beneath an old blanket. The others got in and they quickly drove off. Two men sat up front with one of them driving, her abductor in the rear to watch the feisty little dame for signs of her coming to.

She wouldn't be out too long, but even with the roundabout trip they would make, it would be long enough to get her where she had to be before dark.

+++

Robert Ackers was more tired than he thought. He had set his alarm, but either forgot to pull out the pin or had accidentally hit the arm on top that silenced the bell. It never went off, so by the time he awakened on his own, it was already afternoon. He sat up in bed and stretched, shaking his head over sleeping so long. Looking at the time, he decided it was too late to go to the police station now. He could do that Monday.

Too broke to go out to eat, he settled for whatever he had at home, which happened to be dry cereal and a bottle of cola. He briefly considered mixing them, but that would make a mess. Kept separate he could sit down and put something in his stomach and maybe get some writing done.

"Robert, the food you are consuming does not seem to have any sound nutritional content," Med admonished him. Ackers was surprised that he hadn't heard from Med before now.

Unfortunately, it's all I have on hand. I gave the last of my cash to the cab driver last night to get Sarah home. Banks are closed on Saturdays and I don't have much in my account anyway. I can't afford to eat out today, and while the diner she works at might allow me credit, they'd be closed by now so that's a moot point.

"Yet I sense your energy level is still quite low, and I too am having trouble recharging mine because of that. The fact that you have yet to go outside today and allow me to recharge under the solar radiation of your planetary system's yellow star is also unhelpful. Is there no other way to get sustenance here? Could you not go ask your landlady for another meal?"

Ackers groaned at the thought. *Yeah Med, I could but won't because that would be begging. She's not a wealthy woman, so it was nice enough that she invited us over to dinner, but that meal had to set her back some. Besides, right now what I need to do is write. That's what pays the bills and keeps food on hand. I can't buy food without money, and if you haven't noticed, no one is paying me to play hero.*

The medallion was silent for a while and the typewriter keys began to tap. Then it interrupted Robert once more.

"I will have to consider this problem of yours Robert. You and I working together are needed here to make a difference in how well your people live. I am supposed to assist you in keeping others safe, but we cannot do that by sitting indoors all the time. Yet you also need to be paid for what you do in this life. There has to be a way to make this all work out to both our functional satisfactions."

Ackers snorted in derision. *It would be nice if there was a way to get paid for risking my life as Blue Light, but I have no idea who would do that. Nobody has ever bothered to pay me for anything I do, other than writing. These are hard times, but people like to be entertained. Since my stories do sell magazines, the editors always accept them. Right now what I need is some peace and quiet so I can actually WRITE something. So please pipe down Med and let me concentrate on what I need to do in order to get paid. We'll discuss this later, I promise,* Ackers added, and then went back to work.

It was a fairly productive afternoon. One good thing that had come out of his experiences with Med was it provided additional incentive for new stories. Robert got deep into writing another mystery with a bit of a futuristic science fiction element to it and as the hours slipped by the papers began to stack up. He lost track of time as well as a sense of where he was.

Robert was scrolling more precious paper with a carbon sheet between them into the typewriter when a quiet knock on the door startled him.

He looked up at the time and it was already five forty-nine by his clock. Out the one dusty window, the sun was low in the sky. The last thing he needed right now was a visitor. He hadn't even shaved today! Well, it was too late for that. Getting to his feet, he quickly tucked in his rumpled shirt and brushed the cereal crumbs off his slacks before he went to the door just as the knock came again.

"Who is it?" he asked, a little too wary to open it before he was sure of the person standing on the other side. Med was still sitting on the nightstand, so there was no use in asking the medallion to send a tendril out to investigate.

"Only me Mistah Ackers," Mrs. Mondella's heavily accented voice called out quietly. It wasn't time to pay the rent, so she must need something. He began fumbling with the door lock after removing the slide bolt and the chain that helped to keep the door secure when he was home alone. He opened it to see his landlady standing there with a small manila envelope in one hand.

"A very nice young man stop by and ask for you. He give me dis," she said, handing the envelope over. Robert looked it over curiously because it was unmarked with no postage or return address. Just his name block printed on the outside in greasy black letters, which were somewhat smeared.

"Thanks Mrs. Mondella," he said. She smiled and turned to leave. "Oh, and thank you again for dinner last night. Sarah and I had a good time and the food was excellent as always."

She turned back, her face beaming as she held it between both hands in embarrassment. "Oh, is just plain cooking, but you know you be welcome any time, you and your fidanzata. She's a nice girl. Very pretty and smart too. I can teach her to cook like dat," she added before heading downstairs, happily humming to herself.

Robert had learned just enough Italian from her and her husband over the few years he'd lived there to know she was referring to Sarah as his fiancée, but he was too distracted to correct her. The package didn't seem to have much weight, so he wondered what was inside. Since it hadn't come through the mail, it certainly wasn't a returned manuscript or a check—which he could have used right about then. He shut the door and opened the envelope, peering inside.

And then he swore.

There was a note on plain paper, also written in china marker. If he wanted to see his girlfriend alive again, he had to be at a certain lot across town by dark. The street was named and a lot number given, but nothing else. There was a warning that he needed to come alone, because if he went to the police, she was as good as dead.

He would have thought it was a sick joke, except that tied up with a hunk of dirty string was a big lock of brunette hair that when pressed to his nose, smelled just like Sarah's. There was no doubt in Robert's mind. Someone had taken her prisoner to try and get to him. It had to be some kind of trap!

He was going anyway. And he'd appear to be alone—except that he'd also have Blue Light to back him up.

Med, sensing his growing anger and angst, responded even before Ackers crossed the floor. *"Robert, what is it? Your vital signs have all suddenly increased. Are you unwell?"*

No, I'm just— furious and I'm scared, Ackers answered, quickly changing his shirt to something more comfortable to move around in before grabbing up the medallion to slip into an unoccupied pants pocket. *Somebody kidnapped Sarah! They're holding her prisoner in a lot across* town. *They're trying to get me to come out there after her, and warned me that they'll kill her if I call the police. So it's just you and me Med.* He grabbed his jacket and keys. It might be chilly out there at night and since it was dark colored, that would help him blend in.

"*Yet we are both low on energy Robert,*" Med reminded him. "*And this part of your planet is now turning away from your sun for the next twelve of your earth hours, so I will not recharge as quickly as I would have during the daylight hours. I tried to warn you about that earli–*"

Ackers cut Med off. *Do the best you can and save the lecture for later,* he retorted mentally in a bitter and impatient tone as he locked his door behind him. *I don't have the time or the patience for it right now. I have to get to Sarah before they hurt her!* He raced down the stairs and barged out the building door, letting it slam behind him.

"*Understood.*" Med said as Robert sprinted along the sidewalk, dodging people out walking, for it had been a lovely day. No doubt someone would be following him. They must have been keeping a close eye on his place to know where he lived and that Sarah was now his girlfriend. "*I understand why speed is important, but do you even know where we are going?*"

Vaguely. They gave me a road with an address I'm not familiar with, though I know there's been construction of some sort in that area. That's been in the papers. We'll need to find a convenient spot before we get there to go invisible and enter unseen, but right now we have to figure out whoever might be watching me and give him the slip first. What I need you to do is scan around us and see if you can sense someone focused on what I'm doing. Then we might have a chance to ditch him.

Med understood the gist of what it had been asked to do and began to investigate those nearby as Robert continued to pound his way down the sidewalk. It was late for a Saturday afternoon stroll, so not too many people were out and about in his area. Most were at home for dinner. Yet it was also too early for the speakeasies to be open for business, drawing people looking for a chance to hobnob, imbibe, and maybe do a little gambling or hear some music. They mainly operated after dark when it was harder to see the clientele going in and out. Local people and the police often knew of them, but as long as there were no real problems or any planned raids, they were left alone.

Ackers began to cross busy streets regularly and knew that was a good way to get killed. He couldn't keep ignoring the tooting horns, squealing brakes, and shaken fists coupled with shouted epithets because eventually someone wasn't going to be able to stop in time. He almost got hit by two different cars and a delivery truck and came close to causing some accidents. Someone was eventually going to notify the cops and they'd arrest him.

They were about five blocks from his apartment building. The structures around them were getting much taller when Med said, *"Robert, there is a male youth who has been following you at some distance. He has stayed well behind and stopped now and then to pretend to be looking around, but his focus seems to be primarily on you. I believe there is a small side passage that you call an alley coming up that we can disappear into long enough for me to obscure you, though then I will have to allow you to guide me to your destination. As long as I do not have to maintain surveillance, I can manage both."*

Do it! Ackers said, picking up speed as he spotted the alley ahead. It was dark and dingy looking, and it smelled of garbage and other unsavory things but with Med with him, Robert wasn't worried. He picked up the pace and ducked inside, automatically heading for the nearest inset door. He was still well ahead of the young man, who by the time he entered; Med had made Robert invisible to the casual eye. They passed the youth by at a short distance on their way out, but through Med's ability to show him the world around him, Ackers got a good look at the red haired, freckle faced kid. He would not forget that face or the cocky attitude and would deal with him later. Right now he had to go bargain with whomever was holding Sarah.

Can you increase my speed now that they can't see us? Ackers asked.

"I can, but it will drain your energy faster. You have not been properly nourished today," Med replied.

Just do it! It's too late to take the subway and the sooner I get there, the better for Sarah's sake. She must be scared out of her mind and they better not have hurt her, because I'm going to tear every one of those goons apart one piece at a time.

Med did not bother to reply to what it assumed to be hyperbole and instead pumped whatever energy could be spared into Robert Ackers' body. It was enough to allow Robert to double his pace. He raced ahead, dodging vehicles and pedestrians as he wove his way through traffic and the evening crowds at something well beyond human speed. Robert wished he could fly above the crowded streets because he'd make better time, but Med didn't seem to be able to do that. Not at his current energy level anyway.

That waning energy was a concern because no doubt there would be a big conflict awaiting him. These guys seemed to like their guns and Med was going to have to shield him when they opened fire. He had to locate Sarah and get her to safety first though, which was why going into this while invisible was so important. Although time was getting away from him, removing Sarah from the danger zone was paramount before the showdown began.

It was taking too long to get there and Robert was becoming desperate. *Med, I need some other way to get across town faster. There's still way too much traffic down here right now. Can you do something to help me?*

"Can we not take one of those vehicles like the one you sent Sarah home in last night?" Med asked.

You have to pay to ride a taxi and I'm broke right now, remember? I have no money.

The medallion was silent for a few moments while Ackers continued to run down sidewalks and race across busy streets at his own peril, for now that no one could actually see him, they had no incentive to stop. *"Perhaps we can ride unseen if you know which vehicle is going in the proper direction,"* Med said finally. *"You understand this location far better than I do. Choose something and I will help you gain access to it."*

Ackers looked around wildly and spotted a bus that was headed the right way. *Over there,* he said, pointing and Med safely guided him through the traffic to the next light. *How the hell do I get on board? I don't have a pass and they won't open the doors for someone they can't see anyway.*

"You must leap up to the top Robert," Med told him in a firm tone.

Ackers was incredulous at the idea and worrying about being too late to rescue Sarah wasn't helping his mood. *Med, you must be nuts because I can't jump that high!* He retorted.

The idea of being 'nuts' had to be quickly translated before Med replied. *"Since I have no physical brain, I cannot become insane. Besides, you can jump that high with my help,"* Med insisted. *"You must trust me Robert. I will not let you fail."*

Okay— Ackers said and just as the bus began to move, he crouched and leapt. With Med's help he just managed to land his upper body onto the end of the bus roof with somewhat of a thud that almost knocked the wind from him. Med hadn't been able to hold the invisibility and improve his ability to jump without sacrificing something so the landing had hurt like the dickens! But with some scrambling he had made it up and was cautiously creeping toward the front of the bus, trying to see where they were headed.

We've got to keep moving, he told Med. *I need to go East, toward the river.* What began then was a series of leaps from one vehicle to the next, with

Robert continually working his way toward the area where the note said he had to be. Med made sure he could make the jumps safely and that his landings were less painful, but Ackers tended to flash in and out of view as the invisibility camouflage sometimes had to be quickly dropped to make up for the energy drain it caused.

Save some energy for when we get there, Ackers told the medallion. *That's when I'll need it the most.*

"What will you do once you do get there Robert?" Med asked him. "*I can see by your thoughts that you suspect this is some sort of deception meant to capture and possibly kill you, so we will most likely be entering into grave danger with neither of us at full capacity.*"

I'll do whatever I have to, Ackers said stoutly. *For Sarah.*

That was what drove Robert Ackers on, making leaps and bounds above city traffic until he was out in the east side of the city. When he finally hit the ground again and completely wrapped inside Med's mantle of invisibility, he ran as fast as he could toward the construction site looming up ahead.

CHAPTER 20

It was a rundown district on the Lower East Side, not a nice place to hang around. Darkness had fallen over the area but there were watchers all around in buildings nearby. Most armed and ready to move out on a moment's notice.

The corner lot where the new building was going in had been partially excavated after the remains of an older and more decrepit warehouse complex had been removed along with aging tenements and the string of 'Hooverville' shanties that had sprung up around them. The construction area itself was fenced off and left locked inside was a big dump truck for hauling off debris along with a steam shovel that had done the majority of the digging. Streetlights in the immediate area were off for the time being as the electrical service would be upgraded once the building itself went up, but they were a long way off from that.

The big lot was darkly brooding and seemed deserted. The area had a bad reputation for crimes and gang activity. The word had been put out that something was going down here and to stay clear. Most of the street people heeded that. No one was worried about the cops either. That had been taken care of. They'd learn well after the fact what went down—and why.

The girl had been properly trussed, gagged, and hidden. Where she was kept was accessible but supposedly out of the blast zone. That had come by orders from the Alpha through Mr. Beta, who had a safe and comfortable ringside seat in a building off to one side, where he would be able to watch the fireworks to come and make sure things were handled properly. The charges were set at ground level in strategic areas where they could easily be blundered into. Certainly explosions might draw some unwanted attention, but the idea was to get Blue Light quickly into position and then have it careening from one spot to the next while bombs went off underfoot. Nothing and no one could survive that. It would all be over within minutes and the area vacated before fire and police support arrived.

Robert Ackers was mostly an afterthought, though there were plans to take him down as well. He had been allowed to live up until now because he seemed to be a big draw for Blue Light and the girl was what would bring Ackers forth. The entire thing had been carefully orchestrated to rid this area in contention of two of its most aggravating heroes at the same time and if any coppers dared show up, they'd meet a similar fate. It was a dangerous business to be in, but that's the way the world was now. If you wanted to do more than just scrape by, you either fought for ultimate supremacy with every resource you had or you continually watched your back for the bullet, knife, or whatever other method was used to climb the ladder to the topmost position.

The Alpha was determined to see that the competition got the message that there was a brand new kind of underworld leader, one who knew how to manage any difficulties that came along. The word had come down that nothing and no one was to stand in their way. It had been explained to those who needed to know that the intention was to first take over the borough, then the city, and eventually the state; controlling all harbors and any future airports as well as all trucking in and out of New York. The commerce section would insure a steady influx of cash. A few puppet politicians in office would see that the plans being laid now would be carried through.

It was an ambitious undertaking but it didn't end there. Once New York was brought under control there would be additional major cities in other states to conquer. One of the most coveted was Washington D.C., the gateway to control the entire United States.

+++

When Ackers got to the site, all was quiet—and rather dark.

The streetlights in that sector were off but with Med's enhanced night vision he could see there wasn't a soul around, which seemed odd even for this rundown part of the city. The gate guard was obviously making his rounds. Robert could see a flashlight bobbing as the man walked the perimeter of the far side of the lot. Even with that reassuring presence it still felt like a trap. He directed Med to head across the street to someplace where they could take cover and watch for a few minutes but when nothing happened, he knew he had to make himself known.

Remove my invisibility but no Blue Light yet. I'm going in as myself first.

Med sounded alarmed at the idea. *"Robert, is that wise? If they can see you, they can harm you."*

I know but if they don't see me, they will kill Sarah and I have no idea where she is out there at the moment. So for now I need to do things their way. They don't know I have you though, so just keep monitoring around me and get shields up fast if anything appears dangerous.

"I will do all that I must in order to protect you," Med promised as the now familiar ticklish feeling of the invisible shroud came down. Ackers started to move out. *"Once we are inside though, should I not also try to monitor for Sarah's life force? Though my range for that is limited, I might find her faster than you can. I can tune in on her unique biological signature, which is distinct in each of you humans."*

Ackers had only a vague idea what Med was referring to, but it certainly would be helpful to know where to look. *If you can do that and still protect me, yeah go ahead. That way I can focus on just staying out of danger.*

"I am capable of performing multiple tasks of such a low energy drain even though I am currently below half of what is my usual charge," Med related in a tone that almost seemed like boasting.

Fine! Just pay attention to what you're doing and stop yakking in my head and distracting me, Robert ordered dryly.

What little Ackers could see on his own now would have to do for the time being. He had no idea where these people were, though this was definitely the right address. Now that he had been spotted, the man posing as a gate guard came up and quickly frisked him for weapons before opening up and waving him inside. That meant they all knew who he was and that he had been expected. Ackers nodded to the man and walked in, hearing the gate clang shut behind him before it was locked and chained shut once more. Then the erstwhile guard hustled away, leaving Robert alone in the shadowy, roughly excavated lot.

Med give me more night vision. I can't see where I'm going! Ackers insisted.

Med complied immediately and the area lit up with a greenish glow.

It was an excavation big enough for a sprawling complex and some parking in the back. No foundation had been laid yet but boulders and rubble had been dug out and hauled away, with the beginnings of a trench to put concrete forms inside had been excavated all around what would be the basement level of the building. Some of the dirt had been piled along the fence, other piles seemed to have slumped back inside the trench, probably because it had been a dry and warm fall so far. No doubt they were still working on it, for an oversize dump truck was parked nearby, though well off to one side. In the midst of the basement hole was a big steam shovel on tracks with its boom and dipper arms crossed and the gaping bucket well off the ground, held in place by a chain. That looked rather dangerous to Robert but before he could approach it, a man sucking on a lit cigarette in an ivory holder, whose glowing tip marked his progress forward, walked out of the darkness to confront him at the edge of the excavation. Robert warned Med to be ready in case a gun got pulled.

"So we meet at last, Mister Ackers," the calmly controlled voice of normally laconic Sammy said as he blew a small puff of smoke into the cooler night air. "I have to give you credit, because you were brave enough to come here alone. You're also a hard man to discourage, and that makes you incredibly foolish. You've been warned multiple times to stop interfering in our business, as has your big blue friend. Perhaps now you'll take us seriously."

"You're calling being caught in the middle of attempted robberies and having my apartment broken into a warning?" Ackers snapped.

Sammy gave him a sardonic smile. "I'd call it pretty stupid on your part to get involved in the first place. Stuff like that gets guys killed."

Robert Ackers shrugged and put his hands out. *Keep monitoring Med, I've got to stall this guy for a bit.* "Hey, I can't help it if your people keep showing up where I am, now can I?" he said simply, trying to keep the nervous edge out of his voice. "And I have no idea of who you're referring to as my 'big blue friend'. Look pal, I came alone as requested and what I want to know right now is the whereabouts of Sarah Baker. If she's been hurt–"

Sammy cut him off. "She's alive and well—for the moment. Her remaining that way will be contingent on whether you give us what we want in return, without the 'playing dumb' act. And what we want is your buddy Blue Light. You bring that thing here, then we have something to bargain with. Otherwise you don't get to see your girlfriend again outside of the morgue. You savvy what I'm saying here Ackers?" There was an edge to Sammy's voice as he took a final drag of the coffin nail before flicking it off the holder. It dropped to the ground and he crushed it out with one foot.

"Yeah, I savvy," Robert snarled, "but what you're asking me for is something I can't do. I have no more control over where Blue Light goes or does than you do."

"Then you better figure out fast why it shows up every time you're in trouble and get it here pronto." The conversation was over and Sammy turned to saunter off.

Robert glared after him. He and Med could take on Sammy easily enough and also likely the gate guard or whoever that guy really was, but who knew how many other hoodlums were hiding out around the area? There could be dozens, all armed; and with the medallion less than half power, Robert knew Med might not be able to protect him very long. Plus they knew where Sarah was, and he still didn't. What good would it do her for him to get killed on the spot? Then no more Blue Light!

His shoulders slumped and he felt defeated. He turned to scan the area. *Med do you have any idea where Sarah is?*

"Possibly Robert, yet I am not close enough to be sure. I got some indication of a female around that piece of excavation machinery but that was as much as I could determine. I would not suggest you look that way though because I can sense that there are other human life forms in some of the buildings around us. Most seem clustered around what you refer to as windows or doorways. I believe you are being watched."

I figured as much. How do I get her out of there? He assumed Sarah was being held inside the body of the machine, which was the size of a small room.

"That will be difficult because if my brief sense of her is correct, she is high above us and well out of reach. I currently do not have enough energy left to give you additional speed and agility. They will certainly use their projectile weapons on you if you try to rescue her now, and that endangers her as well. I do have an idea that might help us gain some additional energy though. What powers your vehicles on this planet?"

Robert wasn't a driver, there was no need for that in the city, but he did understand basically how cars, trucks, and buses worked. *Mostly internal combustion from gas and diesel, which is made from petroleum. Why, can you get something out of that?* He snapped impatiently, desperate to get to Sarah and move her at least out of harm's way.

"No. Unfortunately petroleum products are too difficult to convert," Med reluctantly admitted. "I was hoping it was some form of electricity, like your apartment lights. That I might be able to tap into because while it is not electromagnetic radiation like the yellow star you call the sun, it does have charged particles that I can use."

I wish you'd mentioned that a while ago! Robert grumbled as he began to walk back toward the gate. Then he stopped and glanced quickly at the steam shovel, which he knew had a boiler for power, and then the dump truck. Wait a minute— All gas and diesel engines do use a storage battery to start them! Maybe we can draw a little something from that?

"It would be worth trying," Med agreed. "I will need more power if I am going to raise protective shields. Where do I find this 'battery'? I will need to actually touch it if this is a storage device."

In cars it's under the hood in the front. I have no idea if that's the same in other vehicles. Maybe you can send an invisible tendril in to look around and I'll tell you if I see something that looks like a battery.

"That would work if you can get me close enough. You will need to guide me though, I cannot always sense a device that is not active."

Robert considered that a moment. I'll walk over that way and find some reason to linger, but you'll have to work fast Med. We've got to get Sarah out of here before any shooting starts because she could get caught in the crossfire. Then we'll go all Blue Light on them.

"Agreed," Med reassured him.

Ackers carefully wandered over toward the dump truck, positive now that he was being watched. He knelt down before it, pretending to tie his shoe. GO! He said to Med. The unseen tendril snaked out and went under the hood. Then Ackers' night vision became the end of it, where he was looking down a virtual scope through the engine of the big truck. I don't even see a battery! Ackers complained in a frustrated tone. It must be somewhere else.

The tendril retracted and then went underneath the cab. "Robert is this it? It seems to have some sort of conductivity," Med said as Ackers winced.

Yeah, but stop touching it while you're connected to me. That hurt! He retorted.

"It does have a full charge and will help somewhat. It will only take me a moment to drain it and then we can go rescue Sarah," Med reassured him.

+++

"What the devil is Ackers doing?" Beta asked Sammy, who had rejoined him in their observation post. They could both see the man ambling over by the dump truck and then squatting down, but could not make out what for in the gloom.

"I don't know, but he hasn't been much help so far. We do have a lone charge over there. I can have one of the boys set it off and that might bring Blue Light in."

Beta was quiet for a moment, and then he said, "The guy who installed them. He told you it wouldn't do damage to anyone or anything that wasn't right in the lot near a charge, correct?"

"That's what he said," Sammy affirmed. "And it shouldn't be too noisy. There will be some ground shaking and dust and rocks will blow around, but no major damage unless you're almost on top of it."

"Do it," Beta ordered and Sammy left the building and passed the word on.

"Blow that charge right near the dump truck where Ackers is standing."

+++

If he had any idea how close he was to several explosive devices, Robert Ackers would not have been so bold. The big truck was just off the center of the lot, parked with its dump body facing the steam shovel. Med had just announced being done with his draining of the construction vehicle's battery and Ackers was casually getting to his feet when Med screamed in his mind, *"Robert, something is happening—run!"*

Ackers knew to trust Med, but had only taken a couple of running steps when Med enveloped him in Blue Light protection. The explosion rippled the ground and then there was a deafening 'BOOM' that instantaneously threw loose soil and other small objects into the air. Ackers had been able to clear the area but the footing was still bad so he went down hard anyway. He covered his head instinctively as his Blue Light outer form was pelted with rocks which he could still feel through Med's hasty job of shielding him. Upon realizing he wasn't seriously injured, he scrambled to his feet and ran for the far side of the lot. Whatever they had launched at him had not only knocked him flat, but it tipped the big truck sideways.

"What the hell was that Med?" Ackers asked out loud, thoroughly rattled. His ears ringing, heart racing, and he was gasping for breath.

"Do not speak aloud Robert, there are men nearby looking for you and I have you invisible right now. It was an explosive device under the soil and it was very close. I felt a charge of some kind coming and I knew that wasn't

"What the devil is Ackers doing?"

anything normal.”

Then you just saved my life! Ackers realized as he stood looking around wildly. *I could use that night vision again.* Med complied and he could see not just the false guard with the flashlight making his rounds, shining it inside looking for Robert Ackers, or maybe pieces of him, but other men coming out of the darkness, armed and grim, though they hadn't set foot in the lot yet. *I wonder if they have the entire place rigged?*

“As you would say, that's a good bet,” Med answered. *“But I cannot detect them until they set it off. Then some current travels in a line to where the explosive is.”*

Lovely! Well let's find Sarah and get her safely out of here, because I have an idea now for taking these guys out, an angry and determined Robert Ackers said.

+++

“So, what the hell happened out there?” Beta demanded in a stern tone from the men who were supposed to have located Ackers' body. They had all seen him tossed ahead and down, but then he simply vanished. The explosion wasn't large enough to have vaporized him, and it would have left body parts and blood that could be seen. There was none of that.

Of the men who had been the closest, one reported, “There was a quick flash of blue and then he was gone behind the dust screen. We couldn't find him after that.”

Sammy and Beta looked at each other. They knew now who had rescued Ackers. Beta turned to Sammy.

“Get your guys out there, away from the blast zones, but make sure they're well armed. This is shoot to kill. We're taking Blue Light down tonight.”

“Won't that bring in the cops?” Sammy said with some suspicion in his voice. The first explosion had not been that loud. As the guy who laid it out had told them, it didn't shake the nearby buildings in such loose soil. Yet gunfire definitely would be noticed. Especially when the Thompsons started popping. Somebody was bound to hear that and report it.

Beta gave him a look that said you don't question the man in charge. “You let us worry about the police and go do your part. If Ackers gets away, he's going to bring them anyway,” he reminded Sammy.

“It's your call.” Sammy gave Beta a frown and a shrug. Then he and the members of his crew who had come in to report filed out. Beta let them go.

When positive he was alone, he quickly packed up his things, making sure his own sidepiece was handy before heading out to the waiting car.

"Downtown," he told the driver as he slid into the back seat. "Take the long way around."

Those low level thugs were all expendable—even Sammy. Ackers really didn't matter that much, Beta could have taken him out long before now if it wasn't for needing to find out for certain where this Blue Light character had originated from. He had his answer now, though it didn't make much sense.

Beta had made sure that no one but these local idiots had seen him and that they'd never know where to find him. What mattered was that Blue Light was kept busy while other matters were taken care of. That had been the plan from the beginning. It just hadn't been shared with Sammy and his inherited gang of two-bit mooks.

+++

Still invisible, Ackers had moved them over toward the steam shovel. There Med was able to confirm that Sarah was present, but she wasn't inside the body of the excavating machine. She was in the shovel bucket at the end of the dipper arm, and since that was well above the ground, it would be a precarious climb. The shovel end had been chained in place to the end of the bigger boom arm to stay up that high when the machine was off, but Robert was doubtful whether it would remain stable with him crawling out there to try and free her. The steam shovel itself was a complex piece of equipment involving a boiler producing steam and was operated by multiple levers and a winch. It was usually run by at least two men, so there was no way that Robert could move that thing on his own. Just starting it would draw unwanted attention and with the possibility of more explosive ordinances in the lot, someone could get injured if not outright killed.

I've got to climb up there somehow Med, but I'm afraid I'm going to trip something and Sarah will fall to her death. Yet I can't leave her dangling up there while I fight these guys or she might get injured or killed anyway. There are men all over the place now and we're running out of time. I don't know what to do! He admitted in frustration.

Fortunately Med was able to appraise the situation more rationally.

"Robert, calm down and listen to me for a moment. This machine is designed to move large and heavy loads, so it should easily support your

weight. I can protect you both if you can get to Sarah without falling. But between keeping you unseen and shielding the two of you from any of those projectile weapons, that will exhaust most of the energy I have stored. I don't know how much I will have left if you want to appear as Blue Light to these criminals."

Okay, then we tackle one problem at a time, Ackers said. *Let's get Sarah out of here and then we'll see what else we can accomplish.* She was the priority, for it was his fault by playing hero that these gangsters found out about her in the first place. The boom was at an angle to the machine body, having its own turntable that it maneuvered on and someone had left it that way. Robert grabbed onto it and boosted himself up, trying not to make any sounds for there were men not far from his position now.

It was hard not to be noisy. The metal creaked and groaned and the chains holding the arms together rattled a bit even under his own modest weight. There were things to scramble over, like the area where the first chain tied the upper end of the dipper stick to the boom, and then the winch assembly in the middle of that big arm. Every noise he made sounded loud even to his still half-deaf ears, and he dealt with the continual fear of either falling or loosening something that would make the dipper bucket drop, hurting or killing Sarah. He was so completely focused on what he was doing to not to disturb anything, that when Sammy's voice shouted from the darkness behind the lot, Robert was startled and almost fell.

"Ackers, I know you're out there somewhere. You do realize what will happen if we don't get what we want. You think that first little surprise was all we have? Think again chump. There isn't a safe place in this world for you now."

Of course the guy was referring to the fact that they basically had the lot surrounded by gun-bearing goons. At least they couldn't see him. A very agitated Robert Ackers was tempted to answer that smart ass, but that would pinpoint his position, making both him and Sarah targets. So he had to shrug it off and just doggedly keep going onward.

He got to the end of the boom and could see that there was a pulley or something between him and the shovel part, which was directly below. The chain that had been used to hold the dipper arm with its deep, toothed bucket snugged up high was not all that heavy, and Robert was worried that his additional weight in there might break it free. But there was poor Sarah, curled up with her hands and feet tired behind her, her mouth gagged so she couldn't cry out. He had to get to her.

"Robert I sense your hesitation and fear. Your vital signs are extremely

elevated. Perhaps it would be best to rest a bit first," Med suggested.

With those trigger happy gunmen hanging around outside a lot that is supposedly filled with explosives? No way! I'm getting her out of here now, he told Med, turning his back to the scene below. Hanging onto the very end of the boom above and getting his feet planted on the pulley housing between dipper arm and shovel, he slowly let himself down until he could feel the back edge of the bucket beneath him. Then it was a matter of turning around without losing his balance and somehow getting inside to free Sarah. She was trussed up in what looked like an extremely uncomfortable position and she wasn't struggling or moving at all.

That worried him. If they had hurt her—

"Remember I am with you all the way Robert. From what little I can sense of Sarah, I can tell you that she is very much alive, just not responsive for some reason. She had been terribly distressed and feeling rather hopeless. I suspect the explosion frightened her so much that she lost consciousness. I do not think she has been seriously harmed."

Thank God! Ackers now stood on the back edge of the bucket, facing down toward where Sarah lay. Here came the final problem. He had to actually get down into the shovel to set her free. This was a big earth moving machine, the bucket deep enough to hold both of them. Sarah was propped up on some soil that had been left behind, near the teeth at the far end. Robert had only one way to reach her, so he jumped down.

Which was exactly the wrong thing to do. As soon as he hit the base of the shovel the pin that held it in place, which had been partially filed off, made a screeching noise and the bucket began to open. It gaped wide and the two of them along with the dirt and rocks within spilled out in a jumble and began the free fall to the ground below.

That's when the shooting began!

MED! Ackers screamed silently as soon as he slipped from the open base of the bucket. *Protect Sarah!* The fall seemed to be either a long one or was happening in slow motion, for they should have impacted very quickly. Most of the dirt and rocks had already fallen past them to pelt the ground below, though some of it was floating around nearby as he descended. A few stray bullets were bouncing off the metal of the machine behind and above them. One or two whumped into something close enough that Ackers could feel the concussion. Likely caught in Med's defensive shielding.

"I have her Robert and I'm drawing her close so I can protect you both. I have slowed your descents, but I cannot guarantee there are no explosives

below us. If one of them detonates, I will not have enough shielding for that."

It was a risk they would have to take.

As Med pulled Sarah closer Robert grabbed her and wrapped himself around her limp and still trussed form. There were more shots being fired in their direction for while they could not see Ackers or Sarah, the bucket being tripped open had told Sammy's crew that something was going on. So far most of the shots had gone astray because it was dark and they assumed Ackers and the girl must be on the ground by now, though a couple bullets came a little too close. Med had enough shielding around them to keep the bullets from doing any damage, but where they hit, they stung like hell.

"I am moving you away from the machine and the projectiles they are firing so they will not land so closely. Once we touch down you must get Sarah out of here Robert, for I cannot properly protect the both of you much longer.

Just give us a safe landing and shield us until I get her somewhere else. But then I'm going back in to deal with them, Robert told Med as the ground drew very near.

The touchdown was a bit hard, but Ackers took it on his own back to spare Sarah any additional harm. She still was limp and unresponsive, though thankfully she was breathing. Maybe they had given her something to keep her quiet? That made him even angrier, and his anger spurred him into action. Taking Sarah into his arms, an invisible Robert Ackers turned and began to walk quickly through the lot, retracing his steps as much as he could recall them, praying that no more explosions went off.

"Open the gate, quietly Med," he insisted as they reached it. A few shots came in their direction as they passed through and he ran with Sarah in his arms.

One thing that was very troubling to Robert, but until then had only been relegated to the back of his mind, was that no police had shown up. While this was not a residential area, someone should be nearby and have heard both the explosion and the shooting going on. Something was very wrong about that. It would bear investigation later, but for now he had to get Sarah to safety.

The building across the street where he had initially hidden had a loading dock out back with a bunch of delivery trucks parked behind it. Nobody was around and all the trucks were locked, but it was easy enough to squeeze past one of them into the shed-like bay behind and find a safe place to hide Sarah. Robert knew he only had minutes before men would be combing the area looking for him, but he managed to find some old burlap sacking to lay Sarah down on and then couldn't figure out how to untie her.

"Robert, let me do this," Med insisted.

Just be careful not to cut her, Ackers warned as Med sent a thin tendril out beneath the rope, giving it an upward facing edge to gently saw through. In minutes she was free, though still unconscious. Ackers chafed her wrists and called quietly to her, but there was no response.

I wish she would come to, because I have to get back there and deal with those jerks. But I don't want her waking up alone here and wandering around in a daze. What can we do?

Med took a few moments to process that and then told him, "I believe she has been given an anesthetic of some kind. I have no way of telling when it will wear off, because I understand so very little about you humans yet. So while I know you do not approve of my being able to assert myself into the minds of others, I feel we have no choice right now. Sarah should respond to the sound of your voice, even if she is not currently cognizant. If you tell her to stay where she is until you come for her, I may be able to firmly implant that suggestion into her mind, so that she remembers having heard your voice tell her so. Would that be appropriate under these conditions?"

Absolutely! Ackers insisted. *What do I say?*

"Whatever you feel would make her most comfortable remaining here safely out of harm's way," Med answered.

Robert took a deep breath and then leaned down. *I'm ready,* he told Med in their mind link. Brushing Sarah's hair away from the side of her face, Robert put his lips to her ear and there was a little tingling feeling as he spoke, which was Med pushing the words down into the young woman's benumbed mind. Ackers said aloud in a low, soothing tone, "Sarah, I need you to keep calm and just stay here. There are some bad people in the area, but Blue Light is coming for them. I have to go watch out for Blue Light but don't worry, I'll be safe. Um— I love you Sarah, so please stay safe and wait for me!" He gave her a little kiss on the cheek, which made her smile in her sleep, and then forced himself to stand up.

Let's go, he told Med in a determined tone, and they exited the shed without looking back. Robert was afraid if he did he'd lose his nerve and wouldn't be able to leave Sarah there. She looked so small and vulnerable!

Med picked up on his thoughts and mood and decided his partner needed both some reassurance and additional distraction. "She should be safe enough for now Robert. Currently I have another question I need you to *answer for me. There are many large vehicles here. Are they similar to that one that we drained the storage battery on?"*

Ackers paused for a moment, glancing around in the dark with Med's enhanced night vision. It was a dairy distributor and there were eleven identical delivery trucks with the company name and information on them. What difference did that make when he could faintly hear men across the way calling to one another as they circled the construction lot looking for both him and Sarah. If they came across the road, she'd be in danger again.

Yeah, I suppose they are somewhat similar, smaller engines though. Why? He asked in a distracted and somewhat frustrated tone.

"Because if we can drain those storage batteries I can get closer to full power!" Med told him in what sounded almost like a smugly triumphant tone.

Why didn't you say so! Come on, we're running out of time here, Ackers said as he raced over to the first truck. Med sent a tendril underneath, found the battery, and took what it needed. Ackers trotted from truck to truck with Med sucking up all the stored power that could be siphoned off. In the end it only took a few minutes and when done, Med was at about four fifths of full power. Still a little low, but that was far better than what they had before.

Are we all set? Ackers asked in an impatient tone as he felt Med withdraw from the last truck. Robert himself felt better as well.

"I am as ready as I can be. How do you plan to proceed?" Med asked.

That was something Robert had been thinking about while Med was recharging itself. *We go back in there cloaked and when I tell you, Blue Light makes his grand appearance. Can you shield me from gunfire when we do appear?*

Med considered that. *"Yes for some time, but it depends on whether they detonate any nearby explosions. That will drain me far faster."*

So we'll have to be careful, Ackers said as he felt the tingle of the exclusion field around him and began to move out. *Let me know if you sense something and which direction it's coming from. You know we talked about having a screen where I can check your power level myself. Put that up too, but don't obscure my vision with it. I need to know just what we can get away with before I try anything.* He sounded far more confident than earlier and in truth that was how Robert Ackers felt. With Sarah safe for the time being and Med close to full power capacity, he was ready to take on these gangland thugs since the police didn't seem to be willing or able to control them.

Retracing his steps while ducking past armed men, a virtually invisible Robert Ackers resolutely stalked back out toward the lot, alone except for Med. He stopped and took stock of the situation, screwing up his nerve for what he knew had to come.

With Med's night vision active, he estimated that at least a dozen gunmen—all well armed—surrounded the place. Plus the hidden explosives. If Med's shielding went down it would become a suicide mission, but it was something Robert Ackers felt he could no longer back away from. Once he made the decision to actually deal with these mobsters, there would be no going back to the relatively peaceful life he once lead. Blue Light would be the enemy every gangland hotshot wanted to take down, and even if he survived this first encounter, they'd hunt him down like an animal.

So be it then. Robert Ackers was already a marked man anyway. Even if he walked away now, he'd spend the rest of his life always looking over his shoulder. No one would be safe around him—especially not Sarah. For her sake, and to assure the well being of all the good, hardworking folks out there who had to live with this constant threat of sudden violence, extortion, and potential mayhem, he'd use the gifts Med had given him to send a message to these powerful and ruthless criminals. If you came to town looking for trouble, Blue Light would see that you found it.

The gate was locked again and well guarded. He picked a likely spot and quietly clambered over the fence, tiptoeing across the soil, nervous about potential explosives. *You let me know immediately if you sense anything dangerous like another bomb or whatever they put below the soil,* he insisted to Med.

"I always do my utmost to keep you safe Robert," Med replied.

They eventually reached the middle of the lot, though they had to dodge a few armed men. Ackers took a deep breath and then checked the screen Med had put up for him. The medallion was not at optimum power but it would have to do. He had to face these goons now or many more people would die.

Med are we ready? He silently asked the medallion.

"I am as prepared as I can be under the circumstances. Yet you are well outnumbered and they have projectile weapons that can produce many multiple discharges quite rapidly. What exactly do you plan to do?"

Ackers gave the mental version of a shrug. *I honestly don't know, but we have to show these guys that we're not afraid of them and aren't going to back down. But I really want to survive it! So we're going to have to fight fast and smart, with every resource we have. I likely won't have the time or energy to direct you, so whatever you can do to support and protect me while I take them down, just do it. Remember that the shots will come from multiple angles and that they also threatened to trigger more explosions. We won't have time to discuss anything so you'll have to anticipate what I need. I hope you can do that— partner.*

"As you would say Robert, I have your back." It was the most reassuring thing that Med could come up with and it made Robert Ackers smile grimly. Another deep breath and then he spoke those silent but very brave words that the medallion had been waiting to hear.

All right Med. Light me up!

+++

Sammy had sent the guys out to surround the lot. There was still no sign of Blue Light and no one had seen Ackers since the explosion. Yet there was no indication that he'd been injured or killed, so he had to be hiding somewhere and when he crawled out of his hiding place, they had orders to nail him good. When the steam shovel bucket suddenly let go, Sammy had ordered the men to open fire but be mindful of the explosives. They were to just try and keep Ackers and his girlfriend pinned down inside the fence, while he slipped back to the building where Beta had been overseeing things to apprise him of the situation.

Sammy wasn't too worried about the police. They'd been warned to stay out of the area and the commissioner was cooperating quite well these days. Not that he had much choice. They had enough dirt on him to bury him for the rest of his life. At least that's what Beta claimed. It must be true, for no coppers had showed up and no interested citizens either. That part at least had been taken care of.

Yet when Sammy got back to the building he noted that Beta's car and driver were gone, and he had a bad feeling about that. Finding the door locked, he swore and pounded on it a few times before checking out some of the front windows.

No lights inside. No car outside. The Alpha's second in command had obviously flown the coop, leaving Sammy stuck with the situation at hand. Something really smelled bad about that and Sammy paused, wondering what to do next.

That's when the commotion started back in the lot he'd just left, where things had been relatively quiet for a while. There were shouts and then a barrage of shots punctuated by yelps and screams of pain and then an explosion. It sounded— ugly.

Sammy was a born survivor. His former boss had gone up the river and word was he had ratted others out and wouldn't live long enough to be tried. This new mysterious boss and his emissary who lead under assumed names made no promises to anyone, so Sammy had only switched his allegiance to this Beta character until things got sorted out. Now he'd been left high and dry.

Sammy had no loyalty to the mooks with him and since Beta had already checked out, he figured he ought to do the same. There were other cities where a smart man could set himself up in business if he was careful and changed the way he looked. He decided it was a good time to get out of New York altogether.

He headed out of the area in a roundabout fashion and then back into the city proper. He'd grab a few necessary things, change his looks, hail a cab, and leave the city for the bigger guns to fight it out, which was how you survived in the concrete jungle when you weren't top dog yet.

+++

When Blue Light suddenly appeared, it caught the men surrounding the area by surprise. How the hell did he get past them? Ackers capitalized on that shock factor and immediately went after the nearest guy. With Med's ability to increase his speed he was on the man before the gun came up. Med plugged the barrel while Ackers took a hefty swing with his other hand encased in Med's shielding, which connected with the chin. That guy went down like he'd been blindsided by a baseball bat.

They were all over him after that. Shots came from all around, both handguns and automatic weapons, mostly Thompsons with big magazines. Ackers was moving fast and pounded them right back, though more than a few too-close shots left marks on him. It was not going to be a simple rout nor would it end quickly, but he kept trying to plow through them anyway. While he was hurting, the adrenaline rush of Blue Light triumphing over these thugs was enough to keep him going.

Ackers was making good progress in knocking men down and out while disarming them when someone fired a sawed off twelve gauge shotgun with a slug into his chest at close range. That was an especially ugly hit that would have killed him outright without Med protecting him.

It still penetrated partway into the heavy shielding before Med could stop it. The force of the slug within was like a blow with a sledgehammer. It cracked a rib, bruising his heart and ultimately puncturing a lung. Ackers went down to his knees gasping and coughing blood into the blue haze surrounding him.

Those men left standing were immediately all over him.

Med made a frantic effort to make Robert invisible and then forced him up and out of the way before the nearest guy could club him with the butt of his now empty Thompson. A tendril wrapped around the gun and it was ripped from the man's hands and tossed away, taking out the guy with the sawed off shotgun, who was fumbling in the dark to reload.

Damn it! That one really hurt! Ackers complained to Med as he reeled away in the darkness, still retching up blood and trying not to get hit that close again. He was afraid if he took another blow like that he'd black out.

"I know Robert and I'm trying to repair the damage but I have lost a lot of my energy protecting you. You need to keep moving because we both must remain active and vigilant!" Med insisted as Blue Light staggered a bit and almost lost his footing. *"You are still partially visible and so they realize you are injured and are now converging on us. This next barrage will be more than I can–"*

Med was cut off as the shooting started anew, and the medallion had all it could do just to keep Robert Ackers on his feet. A hail of bullets at short range came from all around as men called out, "Kill it! Put that Blue Light out for good!" They were emptying their weapons into him now and there was little Ackers could do but hunch around his injury and try to protect his already damaged insides.

Blue Light was buffeted back and forth, careening in many different directions as the force of the close up shots pelted him. Med thickened the shielding but had to let go of the healing, invisibility, and the night vision. That left Blue Light dim but easily seen, with Ackers staggering around all but blind, gasping and wincing in pain. Then somebody set off one of the explosives by accident, and while Blue Light was not close enough to be thrown by it, Med's last minute warning coupled with the medallion's efforts to send him in the opposite direction forced Ackers forward far too fast. He stumbled over something unseen and went down, almost blacking out from the pain.

At that point he was about ready to give up and just laid there. Head swimming, groaning in agony he waited for the inevitable.

"Robert, you need to get back up! They will surround us and I cannot

hold them off much longer!" Med was almost screaming in his mind. There was no answer as Robert Ackers' consciousness had finally lapsed into a catatonic stupor where the clamor around him seemed very distant and of small concern. Only the pain filled his mind, for while no shot had actually penetrated Med's shielding, the close and constant barrage had pummeled him like many angry fists and feet all over his body. Robert Ackers was beaten up and bruised. Areas that had been hit more than once were swelling and purpling. He was half out of his mind with the level of physical torment he was experiencing and, other than some moaning, was mostly unresponsive.

Men began to close in for the kill, when there came a sound they were more concerned about.

After a few more shots they all began to withdraw as the police sirens and horns blaring began to gradually drawing closer.

"What the hell? The cops are coming? That ain't supposed to happen. He's hurt bad. Let's blow this place up and make tracks out of here!" one of the thugs said.

That was the signal for the men handling the explosives to hurriedly take their places at the plungers. The first detonation was too far off to be damaging but it threw loose soil and rocks in their direction, making the air hard to breathe and partially covering Ackers' legs.

"On your feet Robert, or we will both soon be buried here," Med insisted as another blast went off, covering half of Blue Light's torso, eliciting more moans of discomfort but little in the way of movement from Ackers.

Since the blasts were not close and no one was shooting, Med took the chance of lowering the shield level a bit further to use whatever energy could be spared to try and lever Ackers back upright. *"I cannot fight these people without your help right now. My energy is far too low. If you want to survive, I need you upright Robert!"*

There was no response.

Med was just about to use the rest of its recovered energy to force Ackers to rise when he sensed the next explosion coming from nearby, and quickly re-shielded. It was quite close. The concussion blew Blue Light off the ground, to land on his back some distance away. He groaned in anguish and lay still, barely conscious, completely defeated, and willing to let death take him. Blue Light powers notwithstanding, inside was plain old Robert Ackers, who had never experienced the sort of brutality these men were used to dealing out.

Med had one last mental prod to try. *"Robert if you die here then so will*

Blue Light, and I will have failed. Then these men will take over the city you lived in. Is that what you want to happen?"

No— Ackers told the medallion through his mental fog. *But I can't take any more of this. It hurts too much.* Even his thoughts were weak, his mind distant behind a haze of pain, weariness, and resignation to failure.

"You will hurt no more if you give up on life, but what about Sarah? Is that the kind of future you wish for her? You know how these men are. They will seek her and make sure she does not live long enough to speak against them. If you die now, she will die later, likely alone and in even worse pain."

Oh— not Sarah! The very thought of her alone facing this mess he'd gotten himself into was the catalyst that Robert Ackers needed.

He couldn't leave her behind in a world that nobody sane wanted to live in. It was enough to bring Blue Light back to the world of the living. Ackers slowly began to stir again and the blue glow around him gradually strengthened, as with some effort he dug out and regained his feet.

The sirens were much closer now.

Oh did he hurt! Yet for Sarah's sake he'd bear that pain.

Meanwhile the gangsters were gradually slipping away. The sound of sirens and racing vehicles were not far off at all now.

I don't think I have the strength left to fight these guys again Med, but if we can just round them up and hold them somehow, maybe the police will take them away. The less of them on the street, the better for everyone.

"Now that is a plan I can potentially accomplish. Let us pool our remaining strength to detain them. We are partners after all," Med said with more enthusiasm than Robert Ackers felt.

United once more as Blue Light, the glowing crusader had a reputation to establish and people who mattered to protect.

+++

In the end a couple of the guys did get away, but Med managed to lasso the rest with whip-like tendrils that dragged them back to where they could be wrapped in Blue Light bonds until the police arrived. They struggled a little but no one was able to break free.

When the first of the police cars pulled up and spotlights began to show across the lot, Robert announced in Med's flat, mechanical-sounding voice, "These are the gang members responsible for the shooting and explosions. Please incarcerate them before they harm other innocent citizens. I have other such criminals to hunt down." And before the amazed police officers' eyes, as they moved in with guns held ready and handcuffs out, the Blue Light simply went dark and disappeared.

"Cloaking you with invisibility used up the last of my available energy Robert, and I'm not sure how long I can manage even that. I cannot heal you or guide you home from here."

Understood. I can get myself home but we have to get to Sarah, so I hope you can hold it that long, Ackers answered with even his mind link sounding incredibly weary.

That was concerning to Med, who was still monitoring his host's vital signs.

"Perhaps if I can draw some energy off one of these police vehicles I can make it that far and do a little healing," Med speculated. There were now a couple of paddy wagons pulling up, which was what the medallion was referring to.

No, don't touch them. They'll need those transports for all the prisoners. Take it off one or two of the squad cars. They can always get a jump start or a ride with someone else.

Later on, it would be surprising to find that so many vehicles in the area of the gang activity had dead batteries. It was speculated that the explosions must have somehow damaged them. But the energy that Med drew was enough to heal Robert Ackers sufficiently that he was able to half carry a partially awake but still woozy Sarah Baker out of the area until they could find a taxi.

"I waited for you like you told me," she said to Robert in a dazed sounding voice as he asked the driver to take them to the nearest hospital.

"I'm glad you did," Ackers said, holding her close all the way.

EPILOGUE

Things were fairly quiet after that hellish night.

Sarah had little memory of what had transpired other than somehow she had fainted on her way home and woke up in a strange place that night. It was just as well that she couldn't recall what had happened to her. Before they released her, the emergency room docs said she must have ingested something tainted that caused her to pass out and that she needed to take it easy for a while. Yet at her insistence that she was fine and just needed more sleep, Robert took her home. He remained on guard outside the building she lived in until the sun came up, and then he too went home and slept.

Med had been able to repair Robert's bodily injuries, but Ackers refused to talk about that night. He was still somewhat upset that he hadn't been very heroic after all, and embarrassed that he'd been ready to give up his life so easily. He buried himself in his writing when he wasn't at the diner watching Sarah or walking her home. He refused to read the newspapers accounts of what had occurred or listen to what people were saying. Any internal conversation that Med tried to invoke was quickly shut down, though he continued to carry the medallion with him wherever he went. He was worried about gang reprisals, but thankfully things seemed to have calmed down

About a week later he was sitting in his usual booth waiting for Sarah to get off work when he overheard a conversation at a nearby table about the big gangland shooting. Two men and a woman were discussing it over pie and coffee, and one of them was reading bits from a newspaper. It was worrisome, but didn't sound like it had happened on the end of town where he and Sarah had been. When the others exited and Mildred was clearing their table, Ackers saw they had left the paper behind and asked for it.

"Sure hon. They didn't seem to want it." She set it down before him, and he noted it was an old headline from several days past. How could he have missed that? "You want a refill on the coffee too? Sarah will be a bit. She's getting changed so you two lovebirds can go out tonight."

"Yeah sure," Ackers said, half distracted scanning the article.

It seemed that on the very night Sarah had been kidnapped and taken cross town, while Blue Light was fighting the two-bit gang in that lot, there had been an ugly incident on the other side of the city. A big party at an exclusive restaurant where the heads of many crime families were gathered was shot up. Many of the leading mafia family members were badly injured or killed along with some innocent bystanders. The police were busy in other areas at the time, where they'd been tipped off that some sort of altercation was going on, so they never knew about the massacre uptown until it was too late. No witnesses of consequence had survived and now people feared it was part of a big takeover by some new and more powerful gang.

This stuff just never ends, he was thinking.

"Which is why we are so urgently needed here," Med remarked in a conspiratorial tone.

I don't want to discuss that now, Robert said with some venom, though he knew Med was right. He folded the paper multiple times and shoved it under the table when Sarah came out. Finishing his coffee, Robert gave her a big smile and indicated he was ready to go.

Med remained silent the rest of that night, but knew that Blue Light would be needed again in the not distant future. Let Robert have his evening out with Sarah. Let him write whenever he could. There would be future opportunities to make the world a safer place for such peaceful pursuits.

THE END

ABOUT OUR CREATORS

THE IDEA –

MARK HALEGUA (1953 – 2020) A long time pulp enthusiast and seller, Mark was a well known presence at many pulp and comic conventions. You could find him in the dealers room selling everything from magazines to T-shirts with pulp covers to CDs loaded with cover scans. He passed away on the 18th of March 2020. Mark had been in poor health for some time. He was already diabetic when he suffered a serious heart attack. He spent several months in hospital and then in a rehab facility; during this time he was diagnosed with congestive heart failure and put on diuretics to flush excess fluid out of his body. Eventually he developed kidney disease and was undergoing dialysis three times weekly. Mark was a big friendly fellah, a diehard Yankees fan with a ready smile and a ready laugh for even the worst jokes. Prior to his passing, he'd realized his dream of becoming a pulp writer when his first story, co-written with Andrew Salmon, appeared in the second volume of *Mystery Men (& Women)*. He had been discussing a full length novel with Nancy Hansen & Lee Houston Jr. at the time of his passing and to honor his memory and legacy, the pair took those rough notes and from them produced this amazing novel.

THE WRITERS –

NANCY HANSEN - An avid reader and prolific writer of fantasy and adventure fiction for over 30 years, Nancy A. Hansen is the author of many novels, anthologies, and short stories. You can find some of her work at **Pro Se Press** where she has a selection of original offerings of novel length under her imprint *HANSEN'S WAY*, as well as numerous short stories that have been contributed to various Pro Se multi-author publications. She also shares a children's adventure series called *Companion Dragons Tales* with co-authors Roger Stegman and Lee Houston Jr.

At **Airship 27**, Nancy has contributed short stories to *Sinbad-The New Voyages* and *Tales From The Hanging Monkey* anthologies, and she has an ongoing series of the very popular *Jezebel Johnston* pirate novels, including a 4 book omnibus. She also contributed to the Airship 27 anthology, *Legends of New Pulp Fiction*.

Nancy has also written for **Mechanoid Press** in their *Monster Earth* debut anthology, and at **Flinch Books** contributed to *Restless: An Anthology of Mummy Horror*. Nancy also has a story in the charity anthology *Lost Children*, which benefits groups that help abused and exploited youngsters.

Nancy has an Amazon Author Page at https://www.amazon.com/Nancy-Hansen/e/B009OGK632/ref=dp_byline_cont_ebooks_3

Her books are also available on Barnes & Noble online and some on Smashwords.

Nancy currently resides on an old farm in beautiful, rural eastern Connecticut with an eclectic cast of family members, and one very spoiled dog.

LEE HOUSTON JR. - has been a writer and editor practically his entire adult life. After years of filler material for various community newspapers, he has been with Pro Se Press since the company's inception in 2010 as the writer-creator of *Hugh Monn, Private Detective* and *Alpha* the superhero, with several other short stories as well as working on past anthology magazines for them. While his complete bibliography can be found on his Amazon author's page, Lee's other creative credits include short stories for Airship 27, contributing to and co-editing the *Super Swingin' Hero 1968 Special* with Jim Beard from Mechanoid Press, editing the comic book mini-series *Raye Knight: Spellbound*, from Indy Planet, and serving as the Editor-In-Chief of The Free Choice E-zine (www.thefreechoice.info) since 2005. In what he laughingly refers to as his "spare" time, Lee is an avid reader of pulps, science-fiction, detective/mystery stories, fantasy, and comic books. He maintains contact with readers via Facebook, e-mail via authorhoustonjrlee@gmail.com, Twitter, and his writer's blog at http://leehoustonjr.blogspot.com.

INTERIOR ILLUSTRATIONS

SAM A. SALAS - has been an artist since the 70s. His first love has always been comics and comic book art. His greatest aspiration was to become a comic book artist with one of the major companies. In the mid 90s Sam and a small band of friends decided to publish his own comics. Thus was born ZUB COMICS. The company published two titles. One was GREAT GALAXIES! A science fiction anthology featuring all original stories with art by Sam. The other title was TELLURIA a fantasy title. In all, the company published 11 books and folded in the early 2000s. Since then,

Sam has done various freelance projects for local independent publishers including several stories for a book titled WICKED AWESOME TALES, and a few stories for Ron Fortier. Now mostly retired, he is always ready to take on new projects and looks forward to working with his friend Ron on this new book.

COVER ART

ROB DAVIS - began his professional art career doing illustrations for role-playing games in the late 1980s. Soon he began lettering and inking, then penciling comics for a number of small black and white comics publishers like Eternity Comics—which eventually became Malibu Comics in the 1990s—on their book SCIMIDAR with writer R.A. Jones. Rob eventually began working on likeness-intensive comics like TV adaptations of QUANTUM LEAP and STAR TREK's many incarnations; most frequently on the DEEP SPACE NINE comics for Malibu. At Marvel he worked on the Saturday morning cartoon adaptation PIRATES OF DARK WATER. After the comics industry implosion in the late 1990's Rob picked up work on video games, advertising illustration and T-shirt design as well as some small press comics like ROBYN OF SHERWOOD for Caliber. Rob continues to do the occasional self-produced comic book as well as publisher and designer for his small-press production REDBUD STUDIO COMICS. Rob is Art Director, Designer and Illustrator for the New Pulp production outfit AIRSHIP 27, partnered with writer/editor Ron Fortier. Rob is the two-time recipient of the PULP FACTORY AWARD for "Best Interior Illustrations" for his work on SHERLOCK HOLMES: CONSULTING DETECTIVE and has been nominated for the same award multiple times since. He works and lives in central Missouri with his wife, two children and new granddaughter.

WELCOME TO NOCTURNE, FLORIDA

There has always been something strange about Nocturne, Florida—the City That Lives by Night, It is an entertainment nexus luring tourists from around the world to its nightclubs, music venues and other, more adult entertainment establishments. But there is a darker side to the city which these carefree revelers never see—one of dark doings, violence and eldritch evil.

Now a new sinister force threatens Nocturne and only a handful of unique, gifted beings can protect the city's innocent.

Nightbreaker: a readio star turned vigilante, he exists in a strange limbo world. The beautiful *Dreamcatcher*: who bends all magic to her will. The mysterious *Ferryman*: a living conduit to the world beyond! And their leader: *Black Talon*:the embodiment of the unfettered fury of the African Veld...staling a jungle of concrete and glass.

Together they are *The Shadow Legion*, a secret alliance of mystery men and women who battle the fantastic threats that can tear apart the metropolis they call home!

Their saga begins here in "New Roads To Hell," a gripping novel by Thomas Deja that reveals the secret origins of *Nighbreaker* and *Ferryman*, and features the menace of Rose Red, a crimson-haird devil with a talent for murder!

PULP FICTION FOR A NEW GENERATION!

FOR AVAILABILITY INFORMATION: AIRSHIP27HANGAR.COM

www.ingramcontent.com/pod-product-compliance
Lightning Source LLC
Chambersburg PA
CBHW051125260626
47170CB00005B/1662